SS *PAMPILE* HEADS FOR A WATERY GRAVE . . .

The diesels had been cut to idling so the hydrophones could pick up underwater noises.

'Torpedoes running!'

They were counting.

The time stretched.

Then the yell over the line filled with anger and frustration: 'A hit . . . Herr Oberleutnant! A hit—'

Wolz stared.

The first eel had struck. The dull clang reached through the water mockingly. That was all.

Then—

The sky lit with the blast.

A tall streak of orange-lit foam climbed at the side of the freighter. It hung like a finger of doom, then broke and toppled as the sullen concussion roared in. The flames over there grew. The noise echoed and rang in their heads.

Sea Wolf:
Shark Hunt

BRUNO KRAUSS

SPHERE BOOKS LIMITED
30/32 Gray's Inn Road, London WC1X 8JL

First published in Great Britain by
Sphere Books Ltd 1980
Copyright © Bruno Krauss 1980

TRADE
MARK

Set in Linotype Pilgrim
Printed in Great Britain by
William Collins Sons & Co Ltd
Glasgow

CHAPTER ONE

Oberleutnant zur See Baldur Wolz peered through the Kondor's perspex canopy as the British freighter burst like a jack-in-the box out of the whirls of grey low-scudding cloud. The alignment was perfect. Hauptmann Trojer spoke one word.

'Attack!'

The four-engined Kondor swept down in a long gleaming dive. She roared across the freighter at mast height. Baldur Wolz took in all the jumble of sensations, a series of fleeting impressions; masts and derricks, ventilators and winches, the tall thin smoke stack with the streaks of rust, and the figures of men staring up, transfixed in the moment of horrified surprise.

The impression of a grey and brown jumble of matchsticks tumbled in a box flicked into Wolz's mind and was gone as the single bomb fell free.

He twisted his neck around to stare aft.

'Perfect!' yelled Trojer.

The empennage obstructed Wolz's view. Automatically he tried to crane further round. He was a professional watching professionals in another discipline at work, and he was fascinated. The Luftwaffe had come in for some stick lately – that was why he was here – but he had to admire the way this crew handled the big bird.

The Focke-Wulf 200 surged around in the air as the pilot swung her about her victim.

The freighter surged into view as the bomb hit.

Wolz had seen many ships struck by torpedoes.

Now he saw a ship cruelly hit by a 250kg bomb.

The flash was almost lost in the eruption of black

smoke. Pieces of the superstructure flew off abaft the bridge and the smoke billowed up. The Kondor came around in a wide circle.

'She's done for –' said someone over the intercom.

Wolz saw the ragged edges of cloud flicker across that scene, hiding for a moment the tragedy taking place down there, and then once again the weak spring sun gleamed forth across the sea. Grey green that sea, looking like shot silk from up here. But Wolz knew that down there the tiny white flurries marbling the water meant the men in the boats would have a rough ride.

The Kondor slid through grey clinging wisps of cloud. Down there the boats were splashing into the water. The portside boat hung up on the falls at the stern and the bows plunged in to be smashed and wrenched away aft as the ship's way slowly came off. Already the freighter was listing. She must have taken that bomb in her engine-room, smashing and blowing everything apart, shattering her old plating. Now the hungry sea roared in. In only moments she wallowed deep, deeper by the second. Smoke roiled away. The FW200 circled around. But no more was necessary.

One boat got away.

A couple of oars like the legs of crushed beetles feebly splashed at the sea. The boat humped with the dark figures of people. If they were not picked up they would have a long pull. The Kondor was almost at the extreme distance her enormous range allowed her, far outdistancing any English aircraft of Coastal Command, and Wolz could feel for those seamen down there.

The ship was going.

Quick, it had been, shatteringly quick. She folded up in the middle. Bows and stern rose into the air. Steam and smoke gushed. The bows vanished. Moments later the stern disappeared in a boiling swirl of white water.

The earphones clamped to Wolz's head crackled.

'Excellent! Eight thousand tons – I make her eight thousand.'

6

Trojer looked across at Wolz and his teeth showed.

Wolz would have reckoned the freighter at just under five thousand; but he was in no mood to argue. As a Kriegsmarine officer of the U-boat arm, he was here as an observer on the one hand, and as an adviser on the other, and he knew well enough these Luftwaffe fellows wanted nothing to do with his advice.

'An excellent attack –' he said.

'That's the way to do it.' Trojer sat back, quite clearly bubbling with enthusiasm. 'The Luftwaffe can sink ships. my dear Wolz, very easily. One 250kg bomb – and – voilà – the damned Englishman is at the bottom of the sea.'

Had he left it at that, Wolz would have understood.

But the Hauptmann, intoxicated with the victory, the speed and suddenness of it, went on.

'One bomb – how much cheaper and more elegant than a spread of torpedoes from a U-boat! Hein? You must admit that!'

'Well –'

'This is the modern way, Herr Oberleutnant. Strike from the air! Creeping about under the water – what is it, eight knots? No, no, my dear fellow. There is little the navy can teach the Luftwaffe about sinking ships.'

Wolz shut his eyes. He was a guest here, although on orders, and he could quite see the other's point of view. It had been put to him – albeit in a more comradely way – by Cousin Manfred. Manfred was a fighter pilot, flinging his Bf 109 about the sky as though he rode a prancing white charger, and no doubt shooting down Spitfires by the dozen. The army had won their victories in France, and the Luftwaffe had ably supported them. Although – Manfred had been damned reticent about the experiences he'd had flying over England in the autumn of last year. Rumours circulated thick and fast, and a number of Manfred's friends were no longer around.

Still, despite all the Luftwaffe could say, Wolz was a U-boat man. Always had been. As the Kondor droned on

7

still continuing her westward course to the limit of her operational range, Wolz decided to say nothing in direct challenge to Hauptmann Trojer. But Trojer and the navigator were discussing airmen's details, course and speed, and the flight engineer was reeling off figures, so Wolz left the intercom open to them as he was bound to do and went back to watching the sea and his own thoughts.

This spring of 1941 was going to bring in an enormous U-boat offensive. Everyone knew it. Donitz had promised new boats and fresh crews and such an onslaught on the English that the Atlantic would be swept clean of British shipping.

There had been some difficulty in actually finding the convoys. In this modern war where science played so vital a part, Wolz was as well aware as the next U-boat skipper that the German and the English scientific establishments were pitting their brains and skills against each other in a war which, although not a shooting war, was a struggle no less fierce.

This Kondor operation, now. His instructions were to assist the Luftwaffe people, and to learn of their difficulties at first hand. Their job was to find convoys. Then the U-boats would gather and the wolf-packs would rip and rend the convoys and send them to the bottom.

Only – it hadn't been working like that.

In fact, U-boats had been contacting convoys and homing the FW200os on to them.

That freighter they had just sunk – she had been a straggler. And where there was a straggler there would be a convoy somewhere. Over the horizon's rim, bafflingly hidden by the cloud, a mass of ships was trudging along, in ordered formation, surrounded by destroyers, plunging on over the waves.

But, for all the Kondor crew could see, the convoy might be anywhere.

Long and careful scrutiny of that tumbling waste of waters revealed not the slightest sign of the enemy.

The time approached when the Kondor must turn and with more than half an eye to the state of her fuel reserves begin the long haul back to base. There had been a move to call the FW200 the 'Kurier'; but everyone referred to them as Kondors, and that was that. As a commercial airliner worked over to produce a warplane, she was not entirely satisfactory; but she was fast and she had long legs.

Those were the things that mattered.

Her fuel lines ran along her belly and Manfred had expressed concern over that, as well as holding reservations about her gun armament. But no one could doubt the efficacy of the big aeroplanes when it came to sinking British ships.

The pilot was beginning a gentle bank when Wolz spotted a tiny grey hump lifting from the horizon. He stared for two heartbeats, making sure. His practised submariner's eye, for all that he was perched up in a shaking aeroplane in mid air, would not mistake the shape below.

'Ship bearing two points off the port bow,' he said, clicking his microphone on and speaking distinctly.

The Luftwaffe men picked up the sighting at once.

The Kondor put her nose down, building speed, flashed towards the British ship.

The two stripped Lewises, one in each bridge wing of SS *Gandor*, were cared for by Ginger Elphick and Scouse Kemp. They were dissimilar in many ways, Ginger being pale-faced and small, and Scouse being large and sweaty and moon-faced. But they got along, brought together from their normal duties as an able seaman and a steward by the coarsely-bellowed insults of the Royal Navy instructor who had attempted to explain to them the arcane art and mystery of handling a Lewis gun.

Some instructors sagely gave the advice to point the damn thing and squirt and hope the bastard would fly away.

9

The old three-badger who had ranted and raved at Scouse and Ginger had harboured the strange idea that a Lewis gun ought to be used with the object of hitting what was aimed at.

Scouse was pleased at the chance of firing a machine gun. He could feel the vibration through his thick wrists and forearms and he allowed it was a mite different from slinging hash in the stewards' pantry. Ginger figured the Lewis was an opportunity to dodge a certain amount of the never-ending work of scraping and painting.

SS *Gandor* could make seventeen knots – a tidy speed for a vessel built eighteen years ago – and so made her crossing of the Atlantic on her own, as a runner, without benefit of convoy. Her master, R.R. Witherfield, knew darkly that most U-boat sinkings took their toll of runners; but he believed in his ship and once he showed any damned U-boat his stern he would walk away from the bastard.

On the fantail they had an ancient – a very ancient – four inch gun, and the crew might hit the side of a very large barn at spitting distance. Captain Witherfield depended on getting away, fast, in the second instance.

The first instance was simply the luck of not being spotted by a U-boat at all.

Captain Witherfield, florid, bright of eye, immensely dignified in his brass-bound blue uniform, came out onto the starboard bridge wing just as the apprentice shouted.

'Plane! Plane!' Then, remembering, his boyish face brilliant with excitement, he screamed: 'Aircraft dead astern!'

Captain Witherfield rotated his ponderous bulk.

There was an aeroplane, skimming down towards them from a high scatter of cloud. The sun bounced off her and shot a spark of fire across the sea. The alarm went off. Men ran.

Scouse and Ginger panted onto the bridge wings, flinging off the covers, grabbing a drum ready, cocking their guns.

The aft gun crew were tumbling across the deck.

The aeroplane swooped down.

'That's a Sunderland!' shouted the Third Mate, falling out of his cabin door, almost trampled in the rush. He was ignored.

Up on the starboard bridge wing Ginger swung the stripped Lewis. He did everything right, as the old three-badger had told him, with great ferocity, over and over again. He lined the plane up in the sights. Almost he pressed the trigger.

There wasn't much time . . .

Was it a Sunderland?

The First Officer saw the four engines, saw the sleek fuselage . . .

'Condor!'

Everything happened.

Ginger pressed the trigger, leaning back as the old machine gun bucked and leaped, kept the hose of lead centred on the diving plane.

He saw the bullets punching in as the plane screamed past overhead. The noise was terrific. Smoke blew away. The gun shuddered. There was time to fire a full drum before the Condor swept ahead, turning to port. Scouse swung his Lewis as far as it would go and hosed-off ecstatically.

The Condor passed across the ship, fired at in turn by both Lewises, and went straight on.

'Oh, damn and blast!' screamed Ginger. 'Missed!'

The Condor flew on, heading west, making no attempt to bank and turn and roar in for a second attack.

It was all over.

Pretty soon, surmised Ginger with a sourness in his guts, the Captain would make some heavy enquiry. The First Officer would be sharp in his penetrating way. And, as for the rest of the crew, well, when Ginger faced them no doubt they'd be heavy-handed with their so-called funny remarks.

He began to think it hadn't been such a good idea to be picked as Lewis gunner.

Scouse shared many of those feelings. But he thought — although he wouldn't be positive — that he had hit the bastard. The big plane had appeared in front of him crossing from starboard to port, and he'd let fly with sights *on*. He was sure of that.

It was left to the wireless operator, a skinny lad from Ulverston, to point out that the bullets the Lewis fired weren't going to do much damage.

'You want a damn great cannon, mate, that's what you want to shoot down one of them bastards.'

And the crew, shaken by the swift encounter, agreed.

SS *Gandor* ploughed her lonely way on course. For her the Condor had been like a dream, an apparition. Now the aircraft ceased to exist. The only effect of that flashing encounter remained in the cleaning of the stripped Lewises and the buzz that circled the ship endlessly, talk, just talk.

'The controls — won't work — ' shouted Trojer. The Kondor slid through the sky. Wind howled through bullet holes. She was losing height fast. Somewhere aft of them the British ship vanished out of sight.

Wolz could feel the difference in the aircraft. She felt leaden, heavy, and she rocked as the pilot fought the damaged controls. Just what was wrong Wolz didn't know — he had an idea the pilot didn't know, either — but he felt sure they were coming down.

Lindemann, the navigator, was holding his leg and looking stupidly at the blood seeping through the flying trousers and between his fingers. His face looked like the belly of a shark. The plane dropped toward the sea.

Seeing there was something he could do, Wolz grabbed the first-aid kit and started in on Lindemann's leg.

The noise of wind and engines drowned anything spoken outside the intercom; but Lindemann looked up at Wolz and the drugged look in his eyes changed to one of surprised thanks. Wolz began to cut the trouser leg away. The bullet had passed through without striking bone, and Lindemann should be thankful for that.

The pilot nursed the plane. The sea looked so close the grey-green streaks blended into a rushing streak of dun-coloured speed, passing away aft frighteningly.

A yell on the intercom brought Wolz's head up sharply, his bloody fingers gripping the first-aid kit.

Dead ahead through the perspex showed the outlines of a ship.

A single, glanced look, before he went back to the blood and the rudimentary first aid, told Wolz this ship was not the same one they had attacked.

His wide-lipped mouth drew down at the thought.

Rather, the ship that had attacked them . . .

Thinking that, his sharp-featured square face set in lines of angry annoyance that he had to go and get himself shot down stupidly like this, he saw the flicker of flame.

Fire broke through the after bulkhead, flames leaping and curling up, short, jagged, harsh little flames that burned fiercely in the breeze through the bullet holes.

'Fire!'

'The ship—'

'We'll never make it!' screamed the co-pilot. 'We must ditch now!'

'Wait, wait—'

The Kondor staggered on. Flames and smoke enveloped her. Those damned English bullets must have cut those vulnerable fuel lines. At any instant she could explode, go up in a gigantic ball of flame . . .

'Put her down!'

The heat from the flames could be felt. The plane's nose aimed for the sea. Wrapped in fire she plummeted out of the sky.

CHAPTER TWO

The pilot made a masterful job of bringing her in and pancaking her on the surface of the sea. At the last moment a wing tip touched. She slewed. She wrenched herself around and the starboard wing broke off outboard of the engines.

Wolz saw the wall of green water rushing up towards him. He had taken up the regulation position for a crash, as he had been instructed; but the blow when it came smashed savagely at him. He felt as though he had been run head-on into a stone wall. His mouth popped open. His body felt the shock, a succession of shocks as the plane skidded around on the water.

Jumbled sensations hit him.

He saw Trojer being flung forward. He saw the navigator tumbling about like a sack of potatoes. A dural spar came from nowhere like a spear and drove viciously into the face of the engineer. He was shocked backwards, his face a mere red lump, with the gleaming spar sticking out of it like a harpoon in a whale.

The plane rocked and the noise of breaking and rending crashed at Wolz insanely. He slipped on red muck and tried to force himself to rise. The feel of the sea caught him. That, he understood . . .

The Kondor did not sink immediately.

With enormous effort, Wolz got the navigator out of the smashed and crumpled fuselage. Blood seemed to be everywhere. Trojer was standing on the wing, holding on to the fuselage, shaking and shouting and vomiting, one after the other, like a beaten dog. The bite of fresh air braced Wolz.

'Grab Lindemann!' he shouted.

Water sloshed. The breeze blew. Suddenly, he felt the difference. He was down, out of the sky, down in the sea.

There was no time to strike a heroic pose.

Lindemann was hauled out on to the wing stub. There was no sign of the rear dorsal gunner. With a crew of five, consisting of the pilot and co-pilot, navigator cum radio operator, engineer and rear gunner, the Kondor demanded that most of her crew double up as gunners. Wolz looked about quickly, counting heads. With Trojer and Lindemann on the wing and with the engineer harpooned and dead and the rear gunner missing, only the co-pilot was unaccounted for.

They never saw him again.

The plane was sinking.

Spray whipped across. The swell was as low as to be a mere nothing; but on the sinking aeroplane it sloshed them about unmercifully. Wolz spotted the floating section of the starboard wing.

The four big BMW engines were pulling the slim fuselage down remorselessly.

'The wing!' yelled Wolz.

'Lindemann? –' shouted Trojer.

'We'll manage him. We've got to.'

Trojer began shedding his flying gear and Wolz followed his example. The cold was not too severe. Had this happened on the Norwegian leg of the flight . . . !

The broken edge of the wing, jagged, ripped, looked hard and menacing, the silvered alloy brilliant against the dark grey-green camouflage paint. Water slopped against the wing, the breeze just sufficiently strong to throw spray across in a drift of abruptly appearing and vanishing rainbow colours.

There was no sense in hanging about.

Always a strong swimmer, Wolz had no difficulty in crossing to the wing even with the burden of Lindemann. The navigator took one too many mouthfuls of water, and with one hand Wolz held him against the wing as it heaved up and down. He took a quick look back. Trojer was still crouched on the stub wing, inboard of the inner engine. He looked lonely, huddled there, and for a fleeting instance Wolz wondered if the man couldn't swim.

'Come on!' he shouted.

There was every chance he wouldn't be able to hoist Lindemann on to the wing without assistance.

Lighter in the water the severed wing was being pushed along by the breeze faster than the rest of the Kondor. And, in only a few moments, the plane would be gone – sunk. If Trojer didn't buck his ideas up he'd be gone with it.

'Come on, Trojer! Hauptmann! Jump!'

Suddenly, so unexpectedly that Wolz felt the shock tingle through him, Lindemann spoke.

'I – I'll hold on. You'd better go back – for him.'

Wolz gave the wounded navigator a firm pressure against the wing, and then, cautiously, let go.

Lindemann did not slip down into the grey-green waters of the Atlantic. He held on to a shattered fragment of the wreck, his fingers gripped. How long he could last like that Wolz did not know.

'Go on, man,' said Lindemann, and then he gasped and gurgled as a wave slopped into his face.

Wolz was not satisfied.

'Get ready to lift when I do,' he said. He spoke in time with the rise and fall of the waves. He used the tone of voice he would have used as a U-boat skipper to an offending torpedoman. 'Get your arm around that metal – it'll cut your fingers through to the bone.' He took a fresh grip on Lindemann. 'Ready?'

'Ready – '

'Up!'

Perfectly timed with the pendulum motion of the waves and the wing, Wolz thrust hard. Lindemann shot upwards like a porpoise. He got his arm around the splinter and then yelled as his wounded leg cracked against the wing.

'Hold on!'

With a single smooth effort Wolz hauled himself out of the water on to the wing. It floated very well, with water slopping in over the ailerons and running back in wavy rushes, the sunshine laying coloured mosaics across the shining metal. Leaning out, stretched at full length, Wolz hooked his hands under Lindemann's armpits and, once again waiting for exactly the right moment to heave, hauled the man aboard.

Lindemann looked safe enough, huddled half on his side, his arms outflung.

'Don't move about,' Wolz cautioned him. 'I'll be back almost at once.'

'Go on – Trojer will go down –'

'No he won't.'

Wolz slid back into the sea and swam back. The Kondor was appreciably lower in the water now and Trojer's life jacket might not act fast enough to bring the man to the surface out of the suction of the sinking aeroplane.

With a splash and a shake of his head that set his blond hair like a golden helmet flat against his head, Wolz reached the stub wing and gripped on.

'Trojer!'

Then he saw the Hauptmann's face. It bore an uncanny resemblance to mouldy cheese.

Wolz decided to assume this was seasickness and not fear.

'Come on, man! Look alive!'

He eased along past the still warm engine. He had to fend off the lacerated contours of the wing to reach the trailing edge and so crab along abaft the engines to the fuselage.

There was now very little time left.

'Slide down, Hauptmann!'

Trojer made no move. His teeth chattered. His eyes were shut.

Wolz got a knee on to the wing and forced himself up.

'Can you swim? Well it doesn't matter with your life jacket.'

With that – and with a certain savage annoyance – Wolz hauled the Luftwaffe officer off the wing and into the water.

The shock galvanised Trojer.

Instantly he began thrashing about with his arms and legs going every way. He yelled insanely until water slapped him across the face. Then he gurgled in a most forlorn manner. Wolz smiled. He slid in after and grabbed the nearest bit of Trojer available and started to tow him away from the sinking aeroplane.

They were only just clear when she went down.

The bubbling boil of white water foamed and spouted. To Wolz, accustomed to the sight of sinking ships, the fuss the Kondor made when she sank seemed very small beer indeed. Swimming easily and standing no nonsense from the Luftwaffe man, he reached the floating wing and had to repeat the manoeuvre with Lindemann. At last he hauled Trojer on to the metal and then flopped back, feeling the last-minute bruising he'd taken on his shins as Trojer wriggled in sudden panic.

'You're all right now. Just sit still. Hang on tight.'

Lindemann stared from black-smudged eyes.

'All right?' His voice husked. 'We're done for – '

'Done for?' Wolz kept his voice under control. 'Nonsense – we'll be picked up – '

Trojer, spitting water and groaning, rolled over. The wing dipped and surged.

'Lie still!'

'Done for!' shouted Lindemann. The effort exhausted him and he sprawled out again, abandoned to his fate.

With great care Wolz got to his hands and knees. The wing moved under him with a strange queasy sensation; but he was enough of a seaman to be able to stand up and get his balance.

He looked back – towards the east.

'Who says,' he said with an edge to his voice. 'We won't be picked up?'

The ship they had crossed came clear into view, easily visible. The difference in height even by the small amount of standing up extended his range of vision remarkably. Well, he knew about that, all right. That was one of the things U-boat skippers blessed and cursed their low-slung conning towers for.

The other two on the drifting wing tried to stand up; but Wolz would have none of that.

'Lie still! She'll be here soon enough – then we can wave.'

It seemed perfectly clear to him the ship must have seen them as they roared past overhead, on fire, burning, leaving a long smoking wake. No doubt the skipper would have ordered the tiny amount of helm alteration to bring him directly on to the bearing where the aircraft had gone in.

Wolz moved his broad shoulders under the blue uniform jacket. What would it be like to be a prisoner of war? Not good – not good at all. He had had nightmares about that, on and off. Life for him meant going to sea in his U-boat and sinking tonnages. That way, so he reasoned, he would bring this ghastly war to a quicker end. If he was trapped behind barbed-wire . . .

When the stack and upperworks of the ship hove into view he noticed, with the approval of the sailor, that she was not making smoke. She bore on, and soon the dull greyish-black of her hull broke the horizon. She was dead on course for them.

Not altogether idly he tried to fathom out what she was; but the angle of vision, from bows-on, gave him little chance. She was not overlarge, and her masts and derricks were rudimentary. But, whatever she was, she was rescue from this watery waste.

Instinctively, Wolz put a hand to his holstered Walther P38. Stupid – childish – to think of resistance. He'd be dragged up on board on a bighted line and he'd be dis-armed and stowed away down below. If the seamen shot him out of hand he would not – given the stories current – have been too surprised. But, he had many good friends in England and he knew something of the English, and so had never shared the dark beliefs of so many of his fellow countrymen about that remarkable and wooden-headed island race. The tragedy was they were fighting them at all. Everyone knew – the Führer had made it plain enough despite that amazing treaty – that the real enemy lay to the East . . .

Cousin Siegfried, who was rising fast in the SS, had hinted much the same.

Strange, to think he wouldn't see his uncle's schloss and his cousins for so long – and then he pulled himself up. What was he dreaming about? Everyone knew England was finished. Their resistance was merely the last reflexive wagging of the dog's tail. His three cousins – Manfred of the Luftwaffe, Siegfried of the SS, and Helmut of – well, now Wolz was sure that Helmut was of the Gestapo – would see him again and soon after the total defeat of England.

As for all the charming ladies in his life – he refused to think about them. The complications they had brought to his life dizzied him. The wing surged up and down in the sea and he balanced with the ease and grace of a hunting cat on the tree branch over the waterhole – a favourite image for a U-boat skipper – and watched the steamer approach.

And, of course, he'd miss the comradeship of his fellow U-boat men. They'd had some rousing times in the Hotel Beau Séjour in Lorient! As for champagne – it seemed the French had been making the stuff and storing it away just so as to have enough for the heroes of the U-boats. The press called Lorient the 'Port of the Aces' – and a roll call of the names of the commanders in the flotilla was a roll call of men who had scored their thousands of tons sunk.

Well, Baldur Wolz was well up that table. As the steamer grew larger, steaming on steadily, he felt regret that he was not on the bridge of his faithful if worn-out old U-55, peering along the surface sights, a couple of eels all ready to loose.

That was what he ought to be doing – not washing about on a drifting wing after a real foul-up by the Luftwaffe.

There had been many changes over the last few months. He knew – well, he was as convinced as he needed to be – that an important number of the aces had been sunk. Propaganda had kept very quiet on that front. Unwelcome news would be handled delicately. But that last patrol – yes, it had all been a foggy dizziness, filled with the glare of exploding tankers, confusing – but, on that last patrol, Wolz felt that what he had seen could be explained only in one way.

And that way was in a fashion heartbreaking to Germany, near-disastrous, something to be whispered.

He stared at the oncoming ship. The war at sea was going to become more difficult, despite the great spring offensive, and not less.

The skipper of the ship knew exactly what he was about. Wolz waved; but he felt absolutely certain there was no necessity for that and that the captain had already seen them and was preparing to ring down his engines even as Wolz waved.

The ship slowed smoothly, without undue motion in the sea that sloshed the wing up and down. Making a lee created a tremendous difference. The slight breeze from the west, aftermath of the storm that had played havoc with the convoy from which the two stragglers sighted by the Kondor had come, abruptly dropped. The water heaved in a long unbroken curve, shining, unmarked by the wind. The wing bumped the dirty grey, rust-streaked hull. Wolz looked up.

Strange how this ship, which was quite a small freighter, not much above four thousand tons, as he judged, towered above him. The perspective was truly amazing. A rope coiled down. 'Hold on, my friends,' said Wolz. 'You first, Lindemann.'

The navigator wanted to argue that; but Trojer had wonderfully recovered his composure. He and Wolz fastened the bighted line around Lindemann.

'Fend yourself off – and watch out for that leg.' Wolz allowed himself to add: 'We don't want that dropping off. We don't want to put the English to the trouble of making you a peg leg.'

Lindemann smiled.

It was a wan effort, the skin creasing at the side of his bloodless lips; but he smiled.

He went up, swinging a little, was hauled in. He did not cry out.

'Now, you, Trojer –'

'I think not, Wolz.'

Luftwaffe and Kriegsmarine stared at each other.

Wolz nodded.

'Very well. I allow your prior right –'

'Up you go, then. And I hope they give us some of their English rum!'

As he went whisking up the side, fending off with his feet and trying to avoid any unnecessary thumpings, Wolz reflected that Hauptmann Trojer had recovered his spirits wonderfully well.

The deck of the ship presented the sight that any deep-sea vessel would be expected to provide. There was less raffle lying about, and some of the deckhouses looked a little odd; but Wolz was only thankful to have been hauled up out of the sea. Men belayed hauling as he came in over the side. They wore the nondescript blue clothing any sailors of any nation of the world might wear. But they moved smartly.

Wolz frowned.

Lindemann had been carried off and as he slipped the rope over his shoulders Wolz looked down at the drifting wing bumping the plating and the small figure of Trojer looking up, and bellowed.

'Rope coming down!'

A voice at his back shouted. The voice used good German and in a good North German accent – one of the Baltic ports.

'Welcome aboard, mein herr. You are lucky.'

'Very,' said Wolz, turning. He kept his right hand well away from that holstered automatic. He did not want any misunderstandings. His blue jacket was in good condition, although soaking wet, and he'd have to make arrangements to see that it was dried off properly without shrinking.

The jacket formed an obvious subject for comment.

'Not the Luftwaffe? No – you should feel at home. Herr Oberleutnant.'

The man who spoke was short and chunky, with a fierce beet-red face that showed off his startlingly pale-blond hair in a most curious fashion. He wore a blue reefer jacket and sloppy trousers; yet he moved, and he looked . . .

Wolz stared about the ship. He looked at the men, at the way they tailed on to the rope. Then he looked at the short man with the pale blond hair.

'I'm in your debt for hauling me out of the water, Mister – ?'

'Fregattenkapitän Otto Miehle, Herr Oberleutnant – ?'

Wolz closed his mouth.

'A German ship? Yes, yes,' he said, smiling, feeling all the blood rushing to his head, knowing he was making a fool of himself.

Miehle laughed, throwing his head back, roaring his good humour.

'You are surprised? Of course! But we Germans have ships at sea as well as the damned English – '

Trojer was coming in over the side. He must have heard the last words, for he was in command of himself as the Fregattenkapitän welcomed him aboard.

This was all most odd to Wolz.

The ship *was* German. No doubt of it. The men were sailors from the Kriegsmarine's surface fleet. Well, they weren't out here as oilers for the U-boats – at least – perhaps they were? As they were ushered into the deck-house below the bridge, Wolz saw again the smartly efficient way the sailors went about their work. He had served his stint with the men of the surface fleet, and although a U-boatman at heart, he recognised the distinctive flair of the deep-sea man.

'Schnapps is in order, gentlemen,' said Miehle, beaming. It was quite clear he was thoroughly amused at fishing the Luftwaffe out of the sea, and finding with them a Kriegsmarine man as well, a kind of sea-bonus.

Their wet clothes were taken away and they pulled huge white jumpers over their heads after they'd towelled down.

There was no overt mystery why *SS Kiruna* was at sea. But as the genial conversation flowed on, Wolz felt a niggling dissatisfaction. *SS Kiruna* was, of course, merely the cover name for the mission. A weather ship, said Fregattenkapitän Miehle. The Luftwaffe, particularly, always needed timely information on the weather sweeping over the Atlantic.

'And we in the Kriegsmarine are prepared to provide that weather information, and, also, pull the Luftwaffe out of the sea, when necessary.' And Miehle threw his head back and roared again.

Coldly, Trojer said: 'I appreciate your efforts, Herr Miehle. I am in your debt. But three men of my crew were killed in the crash. I do not feel like laughing. You must forgive me.'

He might have slapped Miehle about the face.

The Fregattenkapitän's head snapped forward. His eyes half-closed. A pulse jumped beside his jawbone. At last, speaking in a voice at once hoarse and breathless he said: 'You are right, Herr Hauptmann. It was thought less of me.'

After that the captain excused himself and went up to his bridge.

The survivors proved something of curiosities to the crew of *Kiruna*, and, war being what it was, the undercurrent of amusement at hauling the Luftwaffe from the sea persisted. The Third Officer, a tall man with a shapeless mouth and protruding eyes, very punctilious, made sure they were looked after. He told them the ship was late reaching station because of the gales.

'But we also have to contend with you Luftwaffe people,' he said in his stiff way. 'You're supposed to be informed – '

Wolz, with a half-smile, left them to it. He well understood the infuriated and baffled rage of a sailor when being bombed by an aircraft of his own side. The Third Officer, Bekker, and Trojer argued on. Wolz went out on to the deck where he could get the sea breeze in his face.

The sun was well down now and they steered on into a long brilliantly orange path of fire, flaked with vermilion, the sea a magic carpet of flame leading him on – to where?

What was he doing sitting uselessly about in a disguised German supply and weather ship here? He should be on the bridge of his U-boat. Well, he walked forward to the fo'c's'le in deep thought, well U-55 had taken enough hard knocks to make a refit essential. Hence his presence in the ill-fated Kondor.

If that was fate – then fate was, as usual, playing dirty tricks on him.

The cabin steward had promised most solemnly that he would dry Wolz's uniform without distorting or creasing it in any way.

'I was a tailor, Bremen, Herr Oberleutnant. I know my business. It will be a pleasure to work on some real cloth again.' And his slender fingers had smoothed down the blue naval jacket lovingly.

Now he appeared at Wolz's elbow, smiling, coughing, the jacket neatly folded over his arm.

'Your decorations, Herr Oberleutnant . . .'

'Yes.'

25

They had, of course, been removed before the drying and pressing operations.

Well, they'd all have to go back. There was no excuse for anyone of the Wehrmacht – army, navy, airforce – to walk about sloppily dressed.

At least, not in the usual run of things. In a U-boat the style of dress at times tended to the bizarre; this Wolz not only tolerated – he didn't give a damn. He was concerned only that the boat should be operated with the utmost effciency.

He went back to the deckhouse with the steward as the shadows lay long across the deck, rolling steadily from port to starboard and back again to port. *Kiruna* looked like any of the many ships tramping the seas, well-disguised, and if – the fanciful thought occurred to Wolz – they happened to run into a British convoy they could easily slot themselves into one of the columns.

They were flying a Swedish ensign, part of their cover, ready to adopt any nationality that might suit. The odd deck houses shrouded guns. The personnel were Kriegsmarine. Yes, they were out here as a weather ship; but they were also out here for something else. Wolz followed the steward through the opened deckhouse door and ignoring Trojer and Bekker and a few more of the ship's officers, went into the cabin placed at the survivors' disposal.

Lindemann lay on the bunk, out to the wide, his mouth open, his face a little too white for comfort. But the doctor had pronounced him still alive and liable to continue in that condition.

The steward produced a brush with a flourish and gave the jacket a few loving strokes. The jacket bore no shoulder straps, as Wolz was an officer. The two gold stripes on the sleeves were tattered and the star above them in not as good condition as he would have liked; but the jacket was comfortable and, whilst it fitted him smartly, was not restrictive. The gilt metal breast eagle had taken a knock somewhere; but the steward had eased it out so that it looked just about right – perhaps the starboard wing had a fraction more dihedral angle than the port; but a gentle twist put the two wings level.

'Narvik, Herr Oberleutnant.' The steward polished up the gilt shield affixed to the upper left sleeve. The thing always looked overlarge to Wolz; but it had been presented for his fun and games up there, and had been earned, by God!

Then the U-boats' Kriegsabzeichen, in gilt, fixed between the third and fourth buttons on the left side. Wolz did up only four of the five buttons on the right side and the ribbon of the Iron Cross Second Class went with the top fastened button. The wound badge looked as knocked about as he had felt the day he'd earned the damned thing. His Iron Cross First Class was in good condition. So, cloaked in the regalia that advertised to the world just what he was – a dedicated and ruthless U-boat killer – Baldur Wolz pulled the jacket straight and saw the steward lifting his hands, smiling.

The steward made a playful pretence of placing a ribbon around Wolz's neck.

'Knight's Cross, Herr Oberleutnant. I am sure of it.'

Wolz didn't know whether to say a meek 'thank you' in appreciation or to cuff the fellow for his impertinence.

Already, they were beginning to say that when a U-boat went down all those members of the crew awarded the Iron Cross First Class would surely perish.

Then the steward – he was a slight, sandy-haired fellow with a bent nose – made amends.

'It is the Kriegsmarine who will win this war, Herr Oberleutnant. I know.' He lifted the brush again, stroking over Wolz's shoulders. 'And the U-boats – ' He made a face. 'I am thinking of volunteering; but my wife – it is a hard thing when you have responsibilities.'

'Yes,' said Wolz, and with a brief thank you went out on deck again.

The little cabin suffocated him – and he, a tough U-boat skipper accustomed to the stinks and the claustrophobic effects of a boat diving deep!

At the appointed time Kapitan Miehle radioed back to his base the news of the rescue, and so the Luftwaffe and Wolz's flotilla commander would soon know of the disaster and of the state of the survivors.

There was no chance of being picked up – unless Donitz re-routed a boat out here – and Wolz would have to sweat out the cruise of *Kiruna* to the bitter end. That did not please him.

Since he had been abandoned in the sea and had given himself up for lost and been miraculously recovered, he had tended to a fatalistic attitude to life and death. He had felt that he should already be dead, by all the laws, and that, as he was still alive, the laws no longer applied. Anything was possible. But – the anything he envisaged did not include sitting rusting in a surface warship. As for the abandoned to fate idea, he did not count this last little escapade. The floating wing had proved the fates had been for him this time instead of against. On that earlier occasion he *had* been given up for lost. The thought sat heavily on him, and he shook his shoulders in the sea breeze and watched the sun at last slide below the horizon.

Surface ships . . . Yes, they were great, fascinating, wonderfully evocative. At Kiel, seeing *Scharnhorst* or *Hipper* or one of the destroyers cutting a white wake, he could feel the lift and the quick and intuitive sympathy of the sailor. But he was a U-boatman. His father had been a U-boatman and had been criminally run down by a German ship at the end of the last war, sent to drown in his own boat.

These thoughts were not calculated to make him feel lively. Surface ships . . . Again he wondered if his old English friend Dick Mitchell had gone into submarines. They had talked around the subject enough with Wolz taking exquisite care to avoid too obvious remarks about U-boats. He knew only too well how sensitive the English were on that subject.

28

He went back to the deck cabin. The sky was clouding over and a few stars attempted to sparkle out; but the night would be dark and clammy, and should be ideal weather for a ship attempting to escape observation.

The glorious summer of 1940 had passed; and the U-boats had taken their toll of shipping and the tonnages sunk had increased with every patrol. That was where he should be now, back on patrol, setting out to sink English ships . . .

U-55 had proved a good boat and his crew superb . . .

The *Prelude* to Act Three of *Lohengrin*, that had been the start of it . . .

CHAPTER THREE

Hellmuth Freyer, the new Third Lieutenant, insisted on playing his record of the *Prelude* to Act Three of *Lohengrin* on the shaky wardroom gramophone, over and over again.

On the bridge of U-55 as they bucked into the chop of a stiff north westerly, Baldur Wolz could not really hear the music over the sound of the sea and the wind and the steady rumble of the diesels; but the music was there, in his head.

He quite liked Wagner, although not given to the excesses of abandonment of some of his friends. He had high hopes of Hellmuth Freyer, who was the replacement for Neitzel, who had cracked on that last fraught mission.

Neitzel had cracked in more ways than one, for Ludwig Riepold, the Second Lieutenant, had been forced to strike Neitzel. Under depth-charge attack Neitzel had attempted to climb the ladder and open the conning tower hatch. He could never have done so, of course, against the pressure of water. But his crazy antics had to be stopped, and Riepold had stopped them. Neitzel had cracked his head against the metal ladder,

As he peered through the flying muck with the wind and water biting into his face, Wolz remembered what he'd said.

'If you've killed him, Ludwig,' he'd said, savagely, as the boat rolled and the concussions smashed at their hull, 'he died in action . . .'

Well, he hadn't died. Now they had a new Third and Neitzel was in a white bed, with flowers on the windowsill, and here they were punching out into the Atlantic. Under Wolz's command, this would be U-55's third cruise. The weather was foul all the time. There were many small infuriating accidents that shouldn't have happened, that couldn't be foreseen until they had taken place, and that did happen.

No one mentioned having a jinx in the boat.

They made their daily reports to B.d.U. and received their orders. They vectored in on a convoy all according to the routine, and when they reached the co-ordinates, the convoy was not there.

That happened twice.

Loeffler nursed his engines. The Chief, with his flat-nosed, pugilist's face and his beard that always grew out as the patrol continued into a fiery red mass, was a treasure above price to a U-boat skipper. Loeffler was a man who understood the guts of a U-boat, the heart and sinews. He could get in a bath-tub, so the men said, and pull the washboard over his head and dive her to two hundred metres.

When the comment had been made, one evening in base when the French champagne had been flowing early and the conversation tended to the personal, a Kapitän-leutnant had remarked, disparagingly, that any fool could take a bathtub down to a thousand metres, if he was suicidally inclined.

It had been Ehrenberger, Wolz's Number One, who had said in his incisive way: 'Ah, but, my dear fellow – and surface her again?'

That was the kind of faith the men of U-55 had in their Engineer Officer, the Chief, Kurt Loeffler.

On this trip Loeffler's genius was strained to the utmost. Every link and ounce of energy, every piston and battery, demanded his loving ministrations. He gave them unstintingly; but he, like them all, grew hollow-eyed and pock-marked of skin, bleary, bearded and foul, gaunt like a wolf.

The Sea Wolf, some people were calling Baldur Wolz. They should see him now, as U-55 fought the sea. As to fighting the English – where the devil were the convoys?

That first patrol of the new year of 1941 was not a success, and Wolz happened on his lone kill by pure chance.

The previous patrol had been of so wild a success that these angry days of no pickings at all at first infuriated the crew and then turned them sullen. They had notched up a figure of tonnage sunk that had been corrected by Kriegsmarine records to the impressive figure of 48,800 Gross Registered Tons. To that must be added the warship they had sent to the bottom. Intelligence had confirmed her name as HMS Cormorant, displacement five hundred and ten tons. But displacement tons were reckoned separately from G.R.T.

Fifty thousand – that was the magic figure, and Wolz had missed it by a measly two hundred. Tonnages sunk were what mattered. Donitz had no need to spell it out, although he did in that stark no-nonsense way of his, sharp as a tack, straight to the point.

Well, U-55 had sailed on this patrol with everyone firmly convinced that, this time, they'd notch the fifty thousand mark. And – nothing.

Nothing!

So that when the forward port lookout bellowed Wolz was informed and was out of his bunk, through the wardroom, through the control-room and up the ladder on to the bridge like a weasel in reverse. He pushed his night glasses up and followed the lookout's pointing finger.

Yes – he could see the ship, dark and angular against the star glitter of the night sky, with just the faintest hint of light in the eastern sky to warn of coming danger for U-boatmen. But there would be time.

Time . . .

The ship was a runner, sailing without escort or convoy.

And, if Baldur Wolz knew anything about it, she would

run all the way to the bottom.

'Close up for diving stations.'

'Flood Three and Four.'

He stared across the dark water, seeing that looming shape bumbling along. U-55 eased smoothly on to the course to bring her into just the right position. The British ship continued on course, serenely as though war was a million miles away.

The sea ran jumbled from U-55's sharp prow and washed across the swelling shapes of the saddle tanks. Out in the fresh air laced with the occasional stinging sleet of spray, the smell of the U-boat appeared, suddenly, as the stink it really was. The breeze blew gently. The stars were beginning to pale. The British steamer continued on course.

No need to dive for this one. Surface attack – that had paid enormous dividends in the Rudeltaktik attacks on convoys, and Wolz would use it now, knowing that the lookouts on the bridge of the British ship would never see the low lethal shape of the U-boat hugging the waves.

'Port ten. Steer three-oh-five.'

'Port ten. Steer three-oh-five.'

'She can't be zig-zagging,' commented Riepold, on the bridge now with the skipper.

Ehrenberger was below, as was usual in surface attack, and if the computing table did not spew out figures that made sense to Wolz, he would loose by eye and his own instincts and flair, as he had done before.

'I agree. But she's put her helm over – she can't have seen us . . .'

'No.'

They spoke quiet-voiced, just loud enough to hear each other over the rumble of the diesels and the splash of the sea. The freighter lifted ahead, dark against the sky, and the water ran and gurgled about U-55's prow. Wolz frowned.

It was possible that the lookouts in the British ship had spotted that tell-tale bow wave. Again, Wolz did not think it light enough for that; but, all the same, he would have preferred to have stumbled across this ship on another bearing.

The freighter continued to turn, and Wolz brought U-55 around inside that turning circle, the bows of the steel shark swinging to cover the firing arc, the eels nestled in the tubes, sleek and deadly.

'Steer two-eight-five.'

'Steer two-eight-five.'

The ship straightened on her new course, and Wolz let his cheeks puff out in relief.

'They know what they are doing,' he said.

Riepold was staring ahead over the coaming of the bridge, hungrily.

'They *think* they know, skipper . . .'

'Yes.'

Ehrenberger's voice came muffled by acoustics as he spoke on the line from the kiosk below Wolz's feet. The First Officer had his eye glued to the attack periscope.

'I can see him clearly, skipper. About five thousand tons . . . ?'

'Four and a half or five.'

'Coming on, skipper,' called Ehrenberger as the attack table chunked out the figures.

'Stand by tubes three and four.'

Riepold had his night glasses to his eyes and was sweeping the horizon, doubling up the continual and uninterrupted watch of the other lookouts. Wolz would have their hides if they failed to see anything – anything at all – out there.

Wolz stared at their target. She sailed on, serene, untroubled, her crew no doubt looking forward to the coming of daylight and that many more miles between them and the dangerous waters around the British Isles.

Well, Donitz had been sending his boats out farther and farther west. This beauty was in for a surprise . . .

The attack table gave its triumphant announcement just as Wolz's instinctive calculations told him the

34

moment to loose had come.

'Loose three!'

A few heartbeats.

'Loose four!'

The eels were running. Reports flowed up to the bridge.

Wolz's fingers gripped the coaming. He stared with out-thrust jaw, his eyes brilliant, willing the torpeodes to strike.

The drill was automatic now. The hands knew what Daddy wanted and they knew what would happen if they failed him.

The other half of that equation was darker, much darker.

Everyone knew what would happen if the skipper failed his boat and his crew . . .

The diesels had been cut to idling so the hydrophones could pick up underwater noises.

'Torpedoes running!'

They were counting.

The time stretched.

Then the yell over the line filled with anger and frustration: 'A hit – Herr Oberleutnant! A hit –'

Wolz stared.

The first eel had struck. The dull clang reached through the water mockingly. That was all.

'Those eels!' Riepold raged. He was furious.

Then –

The sky lit with the blast.

A tall streak of orange-lit foam climbed at the side of the freighter. It hung like a finger of doom, then broke and toppled as the sullen concussion roared in.

The blast smashed at the men on the bridge of U-55. Wolz felt the sudden clenching in his guts, and the relief, and that out-thrust jaw moved, clamping shut. The U-boat ran on smoothly. The flames over there grew. The noise echoed and rang in their heads.

Wolz turned to stare aft.

'Keep your eyes skinned.'

'Very good!'

Now was the moment for some English destroyer to come raking up to catch them silhouetted against the flames.

The freighter listed. She jerked, shuddering, and smoke blew away from her stack. She lurched to a quivering halt in the sea.

Wolz waited, circling, and all the time the lookouts stared with aching eyes into the shrouding darkness that, already, was visibly lightening.

In only moments they must dive.

For a moment Wolz felt he ought to dive at once.

But there were things to do, and it was still not dawn, and that sinking freighter had not been with a convoy. Again he turned and scanned the horizon, looking carefully as the faintest of rose-tinges turned the sea into a ghostly spectre, pinkly running, alive with the promise of day.

Struck in the boiler-room the freighter opened to the sea. Flames dampened out; but that was of small consequence to her fate. She went down rapidly. Boats were swung out and the crew made a good showing in abandoning ship. They pushed off. The freighter, broken, doomed, hung for a long moment as though unwilling to plunge into the depths. Then, in a boil of water and a breaking bubble of foam, she was gone.

Still keeping the lookouts continually scanning the sea and the sky, Wolz nosed U-55 in. Standing orders required him to question the master and to retrieve some object that would prove the name of the ship they had destroyed past the possibility of doubt.

They found a drifting lifebelt, and that would do.

A party on the fore casing hooked it in and it was brought up to Wolz on the bridge, a trophy of war.

There was no name painted on the lifebelt.

Wolz smiled.

'Take it below and get to work on the paint. You know.'

'Very good!'

One coat of paint slapped on to a lifebelt would not obscure the name. Not to the U-boat arm of the Kriegsmarine.

Various shapeless batches of wreckage moved uneasily on the sea. Wolz spotted two lifeboats. He bent to the voicepipe.

'Starboard ten.'

'Starboard ten.'

He told Loeffler what he was doing so the Chief would have his engine-room crew on their toes. The Obersteuermann in the tower was primed. Wolz did not care for the thought of a callous U-boat commander bringing his boat up in such a way as to stove in the fragile hull of a lifeboat. Those people over there had a long sail ahead of them. Still, Wolz tried to operate according to the ideals of submarine warfare he had discussed with his father's friends. The course of the war, the destiny of the German people, sheer practicalities, had all combined to make unrestricted submarine warfare a horrific part of the greater horror of war. If there was any danger to his boat or the lives of his crew, Baldur Wolz put them above every other consideration.

Then the ridiculous side of the thought struck him . . . *If* there was any danger!

There was danger for every minute of every day they were on patrol.

That was certain as fate itself.

He peered through the lightening shadows as the first boat bumped the casing. This part of the proceedings had never really appealed to him – he recalled that poor fellow who had gone berserk with a wrench, and had been shot, and there were other unpleasant incidents.

'Don't be long about it, Herr Leutnant.'

'Very good!'

Riepold went down on to the casing. The deck crew carried machine pistols. They were not wholly for show.

The shouts lifted.

'Don't bring him aboard,' shouted Wolz, leaning over

37

the coaming. He was aware of the picture he would be making from down there; the rough, vicious, U-boat captain glaring down and yelling, the white cap gleaming in the first glancing rays of the sun.

When Riepold got back and the boat shoved off and the crew tumbled down inboard again, Wolz took a final look around the horizon and gave the blessed order to dive.

'Well?'

'Wouldn't tell me anything, skipper, as usual.'

'Stubborn, these English.'

They stood for a moment in the control-room as U-55 glided beneath the surface. Everything was in order and everything ran properly and everything was fine – and, everything was a fiasco.

The paint scraped off the lifebelt revealed the name, SS *Pampile*, Liverpool.

The book told them, bleakly, that SS *Pampile* was four thousand five hundred tons – Gross Registered Tons.

And, as the cruise continued, SS *Pampile* remained their only success.

B.d.U. routed them and re-routed them and they sailed obediently to the co-ordinates. They contacted other U-boats hunting around, like sniffing dogs without a scent.

The waters off the south-west coast of Ireland, which ought to have yielded a rich harvest, gave them a nasty fright when a Hudson dodged out of cloud and screamed down for them.

'Dive, dive, dive!'

The boat kicked ahead as the diesels were thrust into top revolutions. The lookouts fell down the tower ladder, each man taking one and one-fifth seconds – or less – to clear the bridge. Wolz went down last. He slammed the lid down as the white water came breaking and foaming in, and his face was drenched. He looked savage.

The diesels cut at exactly the right moments as Loeffler grouped in the electric motors. The boat dived. U-55 went down like a sliver of steel aiming for the depths where she was at home and where she might find safety.

They all heard the sharp crack of the bombs, the concussions and they all heaved sighs of relief.

Their drill had saved them.

The Hudson had been just those vital seconds too slow.

Baldur Wolz preferred to think his crew had been those vital seconds faster.

Ehrenberger found a dark smile.

'I really think,' he said. 'This is becoming a little dangerous.'

Wolz smiled. Just like Kern Ehrenberger – his name was not Kern but that was what everyone called him – a good, tough, supremely competent Number One, he could handle the men and the boat and not cause Wolz the slightest concern. The trouble was, Ehrenberger would be getting his own command soon and whilst Wolz welcomed that, he would be sorry to see his First Lieutenant leave.

When he did, Leutnant Ludwig Riepold would take over as Number One. Riepold had proved to be copper-bottomed, too – he had flowered wonderfully after Wolz had taken command of U-55

And, as he smiled, so Wolz thought of that boil, that oaf, that blot on the landscape, Kapitanleutnant Adolf Forstner.

Wolz had deliberately left Forstner behind, raving and fuming, when he'd taken the crew up to see about U-55. Forstner had never forgiven him, and had tried to have him beaten up, and had suffered a severe blow to the head as a consequence. That might all be in the past now, and Forstner had his own new boat; but Wolz knew with dark foreboding that the problem of Adolf Forstner was nowhere near settled.

So that cruise wound down to a dismal end. As far as Wolz was concerned it had been no recompense for all the hard work and discomfort and – *pace* Ehrenberger

– danger the crew of U-55 had endured.

Wolz could take scant comfort from the generally similar reports of his fellow commanders. The war of the U-boats against English shipping had taken a new and ominous turn. Everything depended on the new Spring offensive. With new boats and new crews they *must* succeed!

CHAPTER FOUR

Fregattenkapitän Otto Miehle laughed his all-over body laugh. His blond hair gleamed in the cabin lights. He was in a jovial, teasing mood, ready to take all the pleasure he could from riling his visitors.

'Oh, yes, my dear Wolz. I perfectly agree. The army and the Luftwaffe take all the credit. The newspapers are full of their exploits. But we know, we sailors, that it is the Kriegsmarine who will win this war against England.'

Hauptmann Trojer rested his elbow on the table, still not altogether comfortable with the motion of a ship instead of an aircraft. He did not look pleased.

'It takes infantry to hold ground,' he said in a dogged tone of voice. 'And Panzers to secure that ground, and we in the Luftwaffe to open the way for the Panzers.'

Trojer looked sideways at Wolz and the other navy men sitting in the cabin.

'I do not think the navy can do those things.'

Wolz opened his mouth, saw Bekker, the third officer, start to speak, and wisely shut himself up.

Anyway, he was tired of this kind of wrangling. Yes, it was still being conducted in a gentlemanly way, so far. But the inter-service wrangling sickened him. As a young man dedicated to doing all he could, at great personal risk, to help win the war, he despaired of the kind of co-operation that was vital. The army and the Luftwaffe had worked well together. So why couldn't the Luftwaffe work with the Kriegsmarine? That was a puzzle. It was all tied up with personalities at the very highest level. Wolz sat silently, thinking his own tired thoughts, as Bekker spoke.

'The situation is really very simple, Herr Hauptmann. Yes, the army and the Luftwaffe can do all those things. But you forget – '

Trojer had been getting thoroughly bored with Miehle and the naval officers.

'I forget that ships can motor over a trench system, or fly beyond it to bomb troop concentrations, perhaps?'

There was a little silence.

Then, breathing a little more heavily than before, Bekker said: 'No, Herr Hauptmann. Just that the troops you fight must eat, be supplied, given transport. We in the navy stop all that. The English will have no transport and no supplies by the time the Kriegsmarine have finished with them.' He spoke with passionate emphasis. 'They will not even eat!'

Trojer looked up sharply and one of the young cadets laughed, too shrilly. The gunnery officer, Leutnant z. S. Dollmann, heavy-set and with a fleshy face, leaned forward.

'Did I tell you about that girl – ?'

The conversation took a more earthy turn.

But Miehle sat back, beaming, quite clearly pleased at Bekker's masterly destruction of the Luftwaffe man's claims. Watching him, Wolz knew the situation was not as clear cut as that. And then Miehle, breaking into the conversation without regard to the subject – to do with the delights of certain establishments in Hamburg – made Wolz sit up.

'And you, Herr Oberleutnant Wolz? You are very silent. Have you nothing to say in defence of the navy?'

'Only that U-boats will win the war, if – '

Wolz stopped himself from going on.

'If what, Herr Oberleutnant?'

He had been about to say if they were allowed to get on with the job and were not hamstrung by – and then he had deliberately frozen out the ugly images in his mind. Inter-service rivalry had been carried too far already. Cautiously, he said: 'If the weather holds fine.'

They all knew that was not what he had intended to say.

Miehle rocked back, his blond hair a golden flame in the lighting – a flame as golden as Wolz's own immaculate hair.

'I see. But I would have to tell the Luftwaffe that the U-boats, whilst doing as best they can, cannot be the decisive weapon.'

Bekker was nodding away, and the other members of *Kiruna's* quarterdeck complement present were quite clearly agreeing with every word their captain said. No doubt he had said it many times before.

'Surface action alone can give us the weight and fire power necessary. *Scharnhorst, Gneisenau,* the cruisers, and the marvellous ships to come. These will win the victory.'

Bekker was looking radiant.

'And *Bismarck*!'

Everyone looked at him.

Miehle nodded, decisively.

'Yes, of course. And *Bismarck.*'

Wolz looked at them, at the German officers crewing a freighter disguised to look neutral, claiming to be officers of a weathership, saw the looks on their faces, and he began to get a warm feeling in his guts.

He could not, of course, say anything.

Particularly, and the dismalness of that dismayed him afresh, particularly not in the presence of a Luftwaffe flyer.

He stood up.

He had previously offered Miehle his services as a watchkeeping officer; but they had been refused. He was not surprised. Routine was established. They wouldn't want to break up the pattern. Wolz had the idea that after a time the undoubted advantages of another watchkeeping officer would be fully realised and taken advantage of.

'With your permission, Herr Kapitän, I would like to go up to the bridge.'

Miehle cocked an eye at him.

Had he asked Wolz for any reason, the U-boatman would have been unable to supply anything convincing. He just wanted to get out of here, and he didn't want to go to the cabin he was sharing with Trojer. Lindemann had been packed off to the sickbay and was coming along nicely.

'Very well, Herr Oberleutnant. You have my permission.'

'Thank you, Herr Kapitän.'

'But,' said Miehle. 'You have not made any comment on my last remark?'

'No. It is difficult for a U-boatman to divorce himself from his own problems. Surely, the war will be won by co-operation?'

Trojer gave a short laugh; but did not say anything.

Bekker looked as though he might agree, but, he, too, remained silent.

Miehle said: 'Assuredly, Herr Oberleutnant. Assuredly. But that co-operation must tend to the victory of the big ships.'

Wolz nodded and found a smile and so went out. He was always amused at the amount of space these surface sailors required; the ladders and companionways and acres of deck – still, U-boatmen could do with a little more space below, heaven knew – just a little more.

The night was overcast with a mild breeze from the nor'west and if that persisted maybe the lookouts might see the stars before sun-up. Wolz ran up the ladder to the bridge and gave a little shiver as he went in. The place was not all that warm; but it was noticeably more comfortable than on the exposed deck. The Officer of the Watch, Rohlfs, gave him a look which implied that he would be tolerated if he kept his mouth shut and did not get in the way, and Wolz nodded affably and went across to the uncluttered bridge wing corner. He could fee the movement of the ship, that long easy roll with the slightest of coincident corkscrews at the end, and he fancied she would be a different proposition in a blow.

The thought occurred to him that the British lookouts on the ships struggling along in convoy or making a run for it must stand at their posts, staring across the unfriendly sea. It was an uncomfortable thought.

They must stand there mentally cringing against the expected impact of a torpedo. Out of the night, out of the sea, at any moment could spring death and destruction upon them.

Well, he hadn't started this war, and if he had his way there would be no wars at all. But it was up to him and men like him, his comrades in the U-boat arm, to bring this bloody war to as speedy a conclusion as possible. That meant tonnage sunk. And *that* meant men must die . . .

There had been no bands and flower-bedecked welcome when U-55 returned from that first cruise of the year.

As to making a contribution to ending the war, Wolz had done little on that occasion.

Donitz had been busy and had not come down to the jetty to welcome one of his U-boats home.

That, when you thought about it, could not arouse any surprise.

Other U-boat commanders had had as lean pickings.

The U-boat headquarters of the flotilla had been set up in the Prefecture. Here Wolz reported. He expected to be ordered out again as soon as the routine checks on U-55 had been completed. The routine was thorough. The men were quartered in the School of Military Music not far from the Place Lorraine. Home leave occupied all minds.

Lindner, the cox'n, whose recent marriage was still fresh and absorbing, couldn't wait.

'Any news, Herr Oberleutnant?'

Wolz smiled.

'She will be all the sweeter, Lindner, for one extra day's waiting. And, mind you give your wife my very best regards!'

'Very good!'

'We're taking the boat across the Scorfe to the slips.'

Lindner beamed.

'Then it's home leave – for sure!'

Loeffler kept on going and as the engineer responsible for a myriad details he was one man who could count on having no rest until his own mind was at rest.

'And that may happen one day,' said Wolz as they walked down the street, tucking their heads in to the rain, walking smartly.

'U-55 is a fine boat – or, she was a fine boat. But she's had some nasty knocks. They'll fix her up for another patrol. After that –' Here Loeffler shook his head. 'I just don't know if I can hold her together any more.'

'Let's worry about that when that patrol starts, Chief.'

'You're right, skipper. But I'd like to get a new boat . . .'

'Prien has U-47 and Herbert Schultze has U-48. They're a sight older than U-55. Herbert Schultze even went back to U-48 to take over from Heinrich Bleichrodt when he took command of U-67.'

'That may be true, skipper.' The rain slashed at them as they headed down to the naval yard. 'But we've had a fair bit of stick. And, anyway,' he added, as much, Wolz surmised, to give a grain of comfort to his skipper as anything else, 'anyway, we can keep going if the target come up, even if I have to hold her together with some decadent American chewing gum.'

Wolz laughed. He didn't much feel like laughing; but it was what was expected of him.

The rain was getting down the back of his neck and he was looking forward to some real coffee as well as the ever-familiar black sweat. A little something in it would not come amiss, either . . .

The number three pump that had caused them a de

of difficulty on the previous patrol was, according to Loeffler, likely to act up again. The dockyard had done what they could; this time the Chief was going to insist on a complete and thorough replacement. He headed off to the engineer's little empire where he would be able to lean on the counter with all the charisma of the Chief of an operational U-boat. Wolz, with great soberness, understood that Loeffler deserved all the adulation he might get. But for him and men like him, the U-boat arm would fragment and crumble and cease to exist.

Wolz was the Sea Wolf, vicious, fanged, ready to torpedo and shell British ships to destruction, wearing his famous white cap. But he was brought to the scene of the action by his Chief Engineer, and – a pious hope – brought away from it by the same man and his engine-room teams.

Hellmuth Freyer had proved himself a valuable addition to the crew and Wolz fancied the man would not stay a third officer for long. Particularly with the expansion Donitz had in hand. But, for all that, Wolz suddenly felt he could not face the *Prelude* to Act Three of *Lohengrin*, or *Tristan*, or the *Meistersingers* – he just wasn't in that kind of mood.

A little Offenbach, now, or Lehar – he turned aside down a cobbled street. The rain glinted on the cobbles, red and blue and oily, rainbow colours. The houses seemed to have pulled their roofs down, their shutters tightly shut against the weather. The café for which he sought, the 'Black Cat', was not too far down. The estaminet was one frequented by German officers who, for one reason or another, had grown tired of their own messes. The other reason, of course, remained the perennial one of the soldier or sailor on active service.

The only patrons were a couple of lieutenants from a coastal battery, three officers from the supplies and stores departments, and two Luftwaffe flak-artillery officers, who were rather the worse for wear. Wolz took his drink across to a side table, away from the zinc-counter; but soon he was in general conversation with the coastal artillerymen and found, to his surprise, that he was itching to be gone.

'Mark my words, Herr Oberleutnant,' one of the coastal artillerymen said, portentously, his face pale and sweating. 'England is finished and there will follow a general peace.'

'Roll on the girls,' said his companion, whose distressing habit of picking the pimples on his chin discomfited Wolz.

'Ah, but, my friends,' said one of the Luftwaffe officers, sticking his booted feet out. 'When we have England where we want her, peace? Oh, no.' He waggled his head as though he was privy to the secrets of the innermost corridors of the Wilhelmstrasse. 'There will be other eggs to fry, mark my words.'

'You,' observed his comrade condescendingly, 'are in no state to pass judgements on the world.'

'I can smell the wind, Willy, and – '

'And I can smell perfume.' He turned to stare hard at Wolz. 'Is it true, Herr Oberleutnant, that our gallant fellows of the U-boats buy all the perfume in the French shops – for themselves?' And he laughed.

Wolz stood up.

No point in smashing the fellow's jaw for him. No point in creating another fracas. Anyway, Wolz's use of perfume was controlled to the point of near-invisibility – or near-non-smellability. The stink of perfume or the stink of a U-boat. You had to make a decision.

'No,' he said, at last, going out into the rain. 'Most of it has to be left for Luftwaffe flyers' whores.'

As he hunched his head down into the rain he reflected that his so-called rejoinder had been crude and particularly uninspired. More, it had been stupid. What better use for perfume than that?

The whole feel of the men, the smell in the air, the sense of loss of achievement – all of it was bound up in this indeterminate conduct of the war. No one seemed to be doing anything apart from the U-boats.

The invasion of England was now, quite clearly, not a part of the High Command's plans.

The consolidation of the continent was of vital importance, and the French had to be handled with kid gloves. Spain was aggressively neutral. Italy was going to do great things in the Mediterranean. Perhaps out there the next phase of the war might be fought. But the uneasy feeling that Germany, having won a great and resounding victory, was still, somehow, not at peace and not at war, made Wolz jumpy. By God! Some of these fellows ought to do a patrol in a U-boat.

That would sort 'em out!

So it was that when U-55 was taken into dockyard hands he was able to go on leave, and he went on leave in a sore-headed way, like a bear, ready to jump at the slightest provocation.

The first part of the train journey was shared with two other commanders and a party of their watch-keeping officers. The moment U-55 was mentioned broad smiles crossed the faces of the other U-boat officers.

'Ah!' said one, a chunky man with his Eisernen Kreuz, First Class, shining away against his blue jacket. 'The Muck Spreader!'

Wolz kept his face composed. He tried to stop any expression showing, any expression at all.

The others laughed, and passed the bottle they would demolish before many kilometers had passed.

'You have nothing to say, my dear Wolz?'

'The fortunes of war, my friend.'

'Surely you have added it to your tally – fifty tons, was it not? Fifty tons of garbage – '

They roared.

Some idiot had loosed a torpedo from U-55 in a safe anchorage and incontinently sunk a garbage scow. The muck and refuse had spread all over the harbour. The stink had lasted for days. U-55 was the Muck Spreader.

Wolz kept his face like a chunk of granite and, seeing

they were not going to get a rise out of him, the others soon talked of other and more important matters. Women, the war, their boats, women – the subjects revolved around loci of immense importance to fighting men.

They were going to spend a few days of their leave in Paris. Wolz hesitated. But he felt the need to get away from U-boats and the sea for a bit; treacherous thoughts that appalled him the moment he realised he harboured them. He pushed the thoughts away and simply said he had business at home. They bid him a raucous farewell.

Luckily for them both, Adolf Forstner had been on patrol. Wolz had no desire to meet the blot. What lay between them was, he felt sure on Forstner's part, a killing matter.

And that, given Forstner's connections, was dangerous.

He went home to his uncle's schloss in a mood he just could not fathom.

The watch was changing on the bridge of *Kiruna*. The officers carried out the change-over with the strict routine of the Kriegsmarine. Course, speed, sea conditions, orders, everything was done in a smooth, efficient style that would, in ordinary circumstances, have pleased Wolz immensely.

He stared out over the sea.

This dark mood had crept on him, he supposed, after he had seen Trudi von Hartstein safely to Unter-Immenslingen by the Bodensee. Her mystery was unplumbed by him. Dressed in borrowed SS uniform he had driven her by a roundabout route. She had vanished into an anonymous house and he had been curtly given a civilian suit and fake papers and told to make himself scarce.

What Trudi was up to he did not know – did not want to know.

He had been on the point of asking her to marry him – twice. On each occasion something dark and mysterious in Trudi's life had intervened. Whether or not he loved her he could not say. She was gorgeous. She had spirit and intelligence, and she was quite clearly involved in something in which she believed passionately.

His cousin Lisl was, so he believed, so far removed from him that any thought of marriage with her was quite out of the question. Her three brothers would not approve, Wolz believed. So, forgetting the happy romps with other smashing girls – Lottie and others – he had decided he would ask Trudi.

And she was off on some desperate adventure and had vanished out of his life.

Out across that tumbled sea lay the convoys ploughing their lonely ways to and from England. Out there were warships hunting for submarines and for disguised ships like *Kiruna*.

He looked down from the high perch of the bridge. How odd to see the water from this elevation! He was accustomed to the restricted view from the conning tower of a U-boat. This angle of vision and the breadth of view always came as a surprise.

'You going below, Herr Wolz?'

He roused himself.

Rohlfs, going off watch, was smiling at him.

'Yes. We're in for a blow come morning.'

Rohlfs made a face. 'She'll corkscrew like a fan dancer.'

'And,' said Wolz as they made their way down towards the cabins of the deckhouse. 'You can't duck out of the weather.'

'Duck out?'

'Right. Not like a U-boat. You can't shelter *under* the water.'

'We can't.' They went into the fug of the cabin, prepared to turn in. 'And I'm glad to say it. The idea of diving under the sea does not appeal to me one little bit!'

CHAPTER FIVE

Nightmares tortured Baldur Wolz.

Against his eyes the infernal glare of exploding tankers beat with an insensate fury. He heard the massive concussions ringing in his head. He tossed from side to side and his sweat slicked the pillow. His mouth hung open, gasping for air in the close confinement of the little cabin he was sharing with Hauptmann Trojer.

He saw the sea painted a lurid crimson. He saw the dark streaks and whirls of blood in the water. He saw smashed lifeboats and the heads of men dotting the blazing water, consumed and crisped in the fire, screaming, screaming . . .

He jerked upright in the bunk, shaking.

He rubbed a hand over his face. The hand came away wet.

He swallowed.

These nightmares never tortured him at sea, in his U-boat. But, here in this stinking freighter disguised as a neutral – he lay there, shivering, unable to sleep, not caring to sleep.

He had seen these horrors many times, and he would see them again – many times yet.

His the brain that planned the kill, his the voice that ordered the torpedoes to be loosed. His the responsibility. He the man who let loose the hideousness of war upon the sea.

Wolz sat up straighter and dangled his feet over the edge of the bunk. He wanted a cigar, one of his fierce black cheroots but he did not wish to fill the tiny cabin with cigar smoke. His head ached enough as it was.

Uncle Siegfried always had a generous supply of the cheroots, and he always pressed a large quantity upon his nephew when Baldur Wolz went back to sea.

Uncle Siegfried had got over his anxieties about his business. He manufactured weapons for the Third Reich and after the enormous success of the Spring of 1940 when France had been knocked out of the war and England, it was generally thought, must make peace, he had been faced with a lack of orders. The Wehrmacht, it was said, would no longer require the weapons of war. The war had been won.

But when Wolz greeted his uncle and they talked in the sombre library with more stuffed animal heads on the walls than books, Uncle Siegfried was bubbling with enthusiasm.

'Of course, I cannot tell you all our plans, Baldur. But we have weapons coming along – well, I can say that it is a pleasure to employ them.'

'I trust the soldiers will share that view, uncle,' said Wolz, perhaps a little too drily.

His uncle glanced at him, short and fiercely, and then he looked away, reaching for his glass on the marquetry table.

'Yes, I know what you mean. But the war is not over yet.'

'I hear Manfred is – '

'Manfred is a young fool!'

'Oh?'

His uncle looked savage. He downed a gulp of schnapps and plunked the glass back so the little table shook.

'He takes too many risks. I have spoken to his Group Commander. Manfred seems to think he can win the war single-handed. His Messerschmitt – '

'A fine aircraft . . .'

'Yes. But the English Spitfire – well, we have talked about that. We have aircraft coming along that will – well, let that lie. You are happy here?' Uncle Siegfried changed the subject of conversation with deliberate emphasis. 'You have everything you require? It is lonely without the children.

'Surely Siegfried will be on leave soon?'

'Yes.'

'And so, uncle, you will go to Berlin then?'

Uncle Siegfried looked away.

'Young Siegfried has friends – they are useful. I do not wish to be a drag on his – activities.'

'No.'

'He is doing very well. Obersturmbannführer – I should say SS Obersturmbannführer, of course.'

'Of course.' Wolz smoked his cigar for a moment. He decided to chance his arm. 'He was talking about the field force of the SS –'

'He was!'

'And, so, I assume he will receive a command?'

'Big things are in the wind, my boy. I cannot speak of them, quite naturally. But they are big – the biggest thing ever seen!'

Wolz did not wish to know, just yet, what that might be.

'He was saying something about Panzers – or Parachute –'

'The Luftwaffe have those, now.'

'So, it *is* Panzers, then?'

'Yes. And we must have better panzers, Baldur. We learned a few things in France. I am doing what I can.'

Just then Uncle Siegfried's new secretary walked in.

Wolz stood up, for although she was only a secretary, she seemed to him to be treated as one of the family. She smiled at Uncle Siegfried and let the smile linger a little for Wolz. Her smile was very fetching.

Wolz stared at her quite frankly as she handed the file of papers across to his uncle.

So far, this Mariza Kalman had been perfectly cool and polite, distant. She wore gold-rimmed glasses and her mousey hair was plaited and curled into a bun at the nape of her neck. Her blouse of some soft white material hung in pleated folds, and her tweedy skirt appeared far more voluminous than a marquee at a circus. And yet – yet Wolz, with his keen sailor's eyes, had not missed the attractive way she walked in her low-heeled sensible shoes, nor the fine shape of her face, the clarity of her skin, without makeup and fresh and unassumingly charming. Mariza Kalman was from Vienna. There was probably Hungarian blood in her, and her eyes, dark, full, were habitually kept half-closed, as though shutting herself off from the world.

Or, perhaps, shutting off the world from her?

He knew exactly what his shipmates would say if they could see her.

'What!' they'd say, laughing. 'No need to raise the old spargel there!'

Asparagus, that was the slang term for the periscope among the U-boat men.

Now she waited quietly as Uncle Siegfried glanced through the letters. He took out his tortoiseshell fountain pen with the thick nib and, settling himself with a grunt began to sign. Wolz watched with a fascination he could not understand.

A mousey little girl – yes, with a nice walk and a nice face – and a hard-headed German businessman. Well, there was no chance now of walking over to see Trudi, and Lottie was getting married and Lord knew where Heidi was. But, this Mariza, now . . . No, no, my boy, Wolz told himself, very severely. Not on your own door-step.

Walking across to the sideboard – it was carved out of what seemed to Wolz to be solid oak, a fancy he'd first realised when he was, oh, seven or eight, and was discovering the difficulty of whittling real ships out of wood – he refilled his glass and then looked across at his uncle.

Mariza Kalman said: 'That would be delightful, Herr Wolz.'

Uncle Siegfried looked up, pen poised.

'What – '

'Herr Wolz has asked me to join him in a drink – '

'Very good. And call him Baldur like everyone else,

Mariza. Here.' He lifted the papers, in a muddle after his sifting and signing. 'Very nicely typed. And fetch me a drink, too. The thought of the Mark Seven gives me a headache.'

Wolz felt the shock – not so much of the way in which his uncle so casually treated his secretary and the casual way of the naming of names – but in the revealing thought that these letters probably contained secret information and would be worth men's lives if the English got hold of them. He shook his head and poured the drinks.

Uncle Siegfried was long in the tooth.

He knew what he was doing all right.

Mark Seven . . . ?

'Thank you, Baldur.'

She spoke in her cool, half-amused voice, taking the drink. Wolz noticed the slenderness of her fingers, the neatness of her nails, the way her hand did not tremble.

'What shall we drink to?'

'To the damnation of the English,' said Uncle Siegfried.

'Perhaps,' said Mariza, lifting the glass and looking at Wolz. 'To the success of our U-boats?'

'I will drink to that – Mariza.'

So, companionably, they drank.

'When are your friends coming in, Mariza?' Wolz's uncle began to think about getting out of the comfortable leather armchair. 'I'll just go down to the village, I think – don't leave anything out for me. I'll eat at Lincke's.'

Herr Lincke was an old family friend, older than Uncle Siegfried, with two sons in the army, and with a farm that was now a god-send. If things got as bad with the English blockade as they had in the last war, friends like Lincke were worth cultivating.

'Oh, they will be in later, Mein Herr. But, you – ?'

'Don't worry about me, Mariza. Have a good time. You work hard enough.' He looked across at his nephew. 'And you could make sure young Baldur has a good time, too. I'm sure they don't feed him properly in those tin cans – '

'Oh yes, of course!'

Wolz blinked.

Already, and no doubt at the thought of her friends coming to see her, Mariza Kalman was smiling much more warmly. Her dark eyes slid away from Wolz. She replaced the glass on the table and, going out, looked over her shoulder, her gold-rimmed glasses catching the light. 'You will come, Baldur?'

'I shall be delighted.'

When she had gone, Wolz said: 'She has an interesting accent – '

'Austrian, my boy. Full of life. But a good worker.'

'How did – ?'

'Old Bekker, the patent medicine man, recommended her. He's retired now – the war's stopped him making his regular yearly fortune. And his son was killed in Poland. A tragedy. So Mariza came to me, and she's a treasure.'

'I'm pleased.'

'Her family are all dead. She's pretty much alone in the world. These friends – well, you'll know most of them – from around here. Nothing to do most of them. If they weed out manpower like they did last time.' He stood up at last, holding to the arm of the chair. 'Well, they'll find a difference, believe me.'

'Perhaps,' said Wolz with an obscure desire to hit out at something, anything. 'Some of them will be posted to U-boats. That would be interesting for them.'

'Quite.'

Suddenly, Wolz caught a quite new understanding on the part of his uncle. He had always thought the old boy was so engrossed with his business, worried about deals, about production, worried about obtaining orders that he had little time for his family. He always made some excuse and absented himself from the Schloss whenever Siegfried invited his SS comrades down. And, on those occasions, it was probably as well that Uncle Siegfried was absent. Absolutely . . .

He thought of Mariza Kalman. She looked to be about

57

twenty-four or five. He felt again that obscure desire to explore in waters foreign to him.

As his uncle, puffing just a little, went out, he said: 'Mind you eat, young Baldur. Things will get worse before they get better.'

That, for Uncle Siegfried, had been a most revealing conversation. Quite clearly something the old boy knew had rattled him. And why should things get worse? As Wolz bid him good night he felt, again, that infuriating powerlessness of the serving officer cut off from knowledge of the big decisions – cut off from them until they were implemented and the serving officer was up to his neck in the results.

Mariza Kalman appeared briefly, smiling.

'Perhaps, Baldur, you would be more comfortable in civilian clothes? Your uniform – do you understand?'

He wasn't sure he did.

'If we are to stay in the schloss, Mariza, all right.'

'I do not think we will be too staid for you. I have heard how the navy behave when they are on shore.'

'Oh?'

But she just smiled her warm smile, her glasses glinting, and went out with a swing.

It was growing dark already and the day outside was fast fading, with a keen wind and a bitter cold rising from the frosty ground. It had been the very devil of a winter – still was. He could imagine what it would be like on the bridge of a U-boat right now, with the grey sea breathing a chill menace, the wind cutting right through to the bone, the eyes aching and sore with eternally watching for the first sight of an English convoy or an English destroyer. Well, he was well out of that now, hadn't been able to wait to get home, and now he was here the schloss was empty – or just about empty – nothing to do but look forward to the friends of a mousey little secretary.

Grumping away to himself he went off to bathe and change.

Only a few servants were left, for his uncle just wanted the schloss kept up to a reasonable standard, and spent most of his time chasing about Germany on business. He had factories in the Ruhr, of course, and he had workshops in many other parts of the country. He spent a busy life. If business of that kind could be called life. It had given Wolz a comfortable childhood after his parents died, and for that he was grateful.

Putting civilian clothes on again was not as strange as he had expected. He chose a conservative grey suit – when he'd last worn that . . . – and dressed with his usual care. Slicking back that blond hair he looked in the mirror and saw the lines in his face put there by experiences he would sooner forget.

Mariza had the run of his uncle's place and she chose to greet her friends in a small room called the Bismarck Room because a bronze bust of the chancellor stood on a marble column in the corner opposite the windows. The curtains were tightly drawn. A fire roared in the hearth and there was a plentiful supply of logs. The furniture had that heavy look perfectly complementing both the weather and Wolz's feelings.

Mariza's friends turned out to be apparently perfectly ordinary young people. There were two men and three girls. Both the men were unfit for active service, and were employed, by their own contemptuous admissions, in office work that, they claimed, was some consequence to the Third Reich. Wolz felt tempted to dismiss them out of hand, save for the understanding that had been growing on him that everyone was not as they appeared to be.

The three girls were charming, glowing with health, two of them quite pretty in a plain sort of way, the third rather more attractive. They were all dressed smartly and with some taste, and belonged to that stratum of society who existed, as it were, in a broad belt of culture and genteel poverty between the gentry on the one hand – the gentry including those merely wealthy – and the working classes on the other.

Drinks were served and conversation took place, and Wolz felt fed up to the back teeth with it all.

One of the men, gangling and with a prominent Adam's apple, on discovering that Wolz was something to do with U-boats immediately began to display his knowledge of the various flotillas.

'Weddigen, of course, is number one,' he said, flicking ash. 'And the second is Saltzwedel. Since they have left Kiel and Wilhemshaven for Brest and Lorient life must be very dull for you up there.'

'Oh, indeed,' said Wolz. 'You are well informed.'

'A cousin in the Administrative Department. But everyone knows. We are all proud of our U-boats.'

Wolz turned away and crossed to the sideboard to find himself another drink.

Presently they began to play a silly game, with much asking of questions and ridiculous answers. The drink had been working. A wrong answer demanded a forfeit. At first Wolz declined, pleading tiredness after his journey. One of the girls, the one with the mole beside her nose, shrugged in mock-annoyance as she failed to answer her question correctly. Wolz had reached the door. His hand touched the door knob.

The girl, laughing, pulled off one of her shoes and threw it at the man who had asked the question, and who was now staring alertly at her.

Wolz halted.

The next question, eliciting no satisfactory answer, brought the pretty girl's scarf off, unpinned from her blouse.

Wolz looked.

They paused on that for further refreshment. A swastika flag, draped in the corner, glowed into the room reflecting the firelight. The cut glass decanters glittered. The other girl threw her second shoe.

Mariza removed the pin from her coiled hair. The hair fell about her shoulders. With a quick, bird-like movement, she pulled out the braid and tossed her head. Her hair swirled.

So it went on.

When Mariza removed her blouse – Wolz felt pretty damned sure she knew the answer to the question all right – she threw it on to the polished table.

'Baldur!' she said, laughing, her hair falling about her shoulders. 'If you stare at us like that – you should join in – it just isn't fair!'

'No! No!' and 'That's right!' called the others.

Wolz stepped towards the table. He was holding a glass.

'Very well.'

He answered the question correctly whereupon they all cat-called him.

'Spoil-sport!' and 'Fuddy-duddy!'

This might very well be a stupid game. But Wolz saw that the undertones were there, clear and unmistakable. Very respectable young people, these, quiet and well-mannered in the normal way. But they had been infected by the same kind of feverishness that made people in wartime behave in ways far removed from what they would consider normal.

The next round of questions saw the girl with the mole slip her brassiere off and throw it at Wolz's head. He caught the scrap of lace, and laughed, and that, more or less, settled it.

His own shirt came off and then Mariza answered a question correctly, and stared at him, wide-eyed, laughing, her colour high and, suddenly, Wolz realised that she was a woman, and rich and voluptuous, and she was working her dark will on him.

And – he didn't give a damn.

The last few garments rustled off with shrieks of laughter, and then the gramophone was put on and they danced, close dances, gliding about the floor, and Wolz had his arms full of Mariza, and he felt very, very good indeed.

CHAPTER SIX

The nightmares gave way at last to a troubled sleep, in which fragments of Mariza's glowing face drifted between the burning hulks of tankers and the blazing, crisping, boiling faces of men shrieking in the water. There was a deal more to Mariza than appeared from her mousey hair coiled in a bun and her gold-rimmed spectacles.

Fregattenkapitän Otto Miehle stumped up to Wolz the next morning. The captain was in a foul mood. A fight had broken out among the hands and in stalking in to stop the fracas Leutnant Bekker had received a black eye and a bloody nose.

'You will take over Leutnant Bekker's watch, Herr Oberleutnant!'

'Very good!'

At least, it gave him something to do, mindless though it might be in the context of the U-boat war.

The days were bleak and grey and yet with the promise of a fine May to come. The sea heaved unendingly as SS *Kiruna* drove on her course. Wolz soon came to the conclusion the ship was following a set pattern. She had reached her rendezvous co-ordinates and was orbiting them and keeping in close touch.

The men involved in the fight were harshly disciplined and Bekker's actions were commented on with feeling. His eye received a deal of sympathy and covert amusement from his fellow officers.

Miehle kept hovering about the wireless shack. He handled a good number of the Commander Only signals and the Enigma machine sitting like a plump overgrown typewriter was kept fully occupied. The ciphers were changed and changed again, and the Enigma chunked its rolls around and clanked out the orders.

Most of them were not revealed in any detail whatsoever, except in the orders Miehle gave his officers.

Something was brewing, and Wolz itched to know what it was.

Of course, the remarks passed at meal times, infuriating in their casualness, had already given him the strongest clues. What, he wanted to know, was Miehle up to in not confiding in the new arrival who was, after all, a naval officer like himself?

The Enigma coding machine was so arranged that it could be swung up on gimbals and drop down out of sight into a recess in the bulkhead. A false wooden door would then fall into position, and no one would ever guess the most modern and efficient of code-handling machinery was anywhere aboard.

When Wolz had been introduced to the Luftwaffe officers just prior to this fateful flight he had been named as the skipper of U-55.

That information was now known to Miehle.

'You had a nasty fright, did you not, Herr Oberleutnant in January of last year?'

'I was not in the boat at the time, Herr Kapitän. I have heard what happened, of course.'

'A Sunderland, was it not?'

'Yes, and two English destroyers.'

SS *Kiruna* rolled on, solid and heavy in the sea, and a fan-dancer when there was any kind of seaway.

'Well, you U-boatmen are to be congratulated, and, also to be pitied a little. I think. For it is clear you are all mad.'

Wolz could take that kind of remark in the friendly spirit in which it was made.

'So they say. But, at the least, Herr Kapitän, we can avoid the worst excesses of gales which you must –'

'Quite. So long as the batteries last out, hein?'

'Just so.'

Miehle took himself off, shaking his head, Wolz continued to stand Bekker's watch, and, he had to admit to himself, even if the duty was mindless it was far preferable to moping about in the ship with no object or aim in life.

One signal came in that made him twist his lips.

Relayed through to *Kiruna* from B.d.U. came the message that Oblt z. S. Wolz was not forgotten . . .

HMS *Bruiser* crashed through the seas, cascading white-flecked green clear over the foredeck to the forward 4.7". She rolled like an eel, and twisted lithely, and sprang free from the clutching seas, and so doggedly battled her way on forcefully at a good twenty-five knots.

Lieutenant Commander Dick Mitchell, RN, was in a hurry.

His orders called for him to be on station at 23.59 and on station at midnight he would be – or know the reason why.

He stood on his little bridge revelling in the swift plunge of his command through the seas. *Bruiser* was a destroyer, a real destroyer, and he joyed in every rivet and plate of her.

She was his – and he was hers.

The Yeoman of Signals came up with a message flimsy and Mitchell read it with a sinking heart.

Then he gave the necessary orders.

'Pilot – make a course that is the shortest you can make it. I'll come down and check with you and the Chief on fuel. Ring down to fifteen knots. Steer two-seven-oh.'

'Steer – two-seven-oh,' came the voice of the quartermaster.

Mitchell looked around his bridge. The night was not too clear, visibility down to less than two miles; but he expected his lookouts to see anything that showed, anything at all, and they understood that expectation.

He had brought most of the crew of poor *Cormorant* with him to his new command. The new hands, HO ratings, most of them, had quickly learned what Ram Mitchell said, went – in spades.

The ship leaned gently against the motion of the waves and her own motion sensibly decreased as the speed came off and she cut the wind more finely. Mitchell went down the ladder, grabbing his duffle coat more firmly around him.

Lieutenant Commander Richard Algernon Mitchell turned his lean jawed face into that familiar beakhead of determination as he went to discuss the best course and speed with the Pilot and the Chief. His smooth face now bore lines that had not been there a year ago. He was still called a maniac, still sometimes referred to as Ram Mitchell. But his men knew he would cherish them. They formed a team, a partnership, and with *Bruiser* they were going to do great things.

Or Mitchell would know the reason why.

Lieutenant Andy Stevens said: 'What's the flap, skipper?'

'New rendezvous, Number One.'

'They'd louse up parking in the middle of Wembley Stadium – ' began Stevens. He took a breath. 'Any idea what it's all about, sir?'

'No. But we'll find out when we get there.'

Andy Stevens was hard-bitten. A short, chunky man he ran the ship rather more like a high-powered electric motor than like clockwork. He got results.

He joined the Pilot and the Chief, who ritually wiped his hands on a chunk of cotton waste, his long-nosed face intent.

'We're supposed to bunker 388 tons, skipper, and we're supposed to have a radius of action of four thousand eight hundred miles at fifteen knots.'

'We're doing fifteen knots, now, Chief.'

'Och, aye. Well, she'll do better at nineteen and a half in this sea.'

Mitchell nodded.

'My sentiments exactly. If you have a knife and can cut through, then cut.' He nodded again to Stevens who gave the necessary orders to bring *Bruiser* up to nineteen point five knots.

Then the Pilot, Sub-Lieutenant Garvin Fellowes, started quickly to work out the elapsed time.

On the bulkhead of the wardroom, in the captain's cabin, in many other unlikely places, pictures hung. The pictures showed what purported to be a ship. Many of the pictures illuminated merely what looked like a long thin log, with a tall thin mast and two widely-spaced funnels, the whole smothered in spray.

Underneath in spidery lettering anyone interested could read: HMS *Bruiser*.

His Majesty's Torpedo Boat Destroyer *Bruiser*. Launched, 1895, speed, 27 knots.

Looking at her, Mitchell had often drawn in his breath and whistled. What conditions had been like in her he did not care to think; they were bad enough in the present *Bruiser*, with water always slopping about the mess decks, with condensation for ever dripping, with facilities for drying the men's clothes non-existent. That old *Bruiser* had been a turtle-back destroyer, with a twelve pounder and a few six pounders and with two eighteen-inch torpedo tubes.

Well, as he felt his ship moving through the sea, and lurching and recovering and battling on, he wouldn't have liked to have been called on to command the old ship and do what he had to do today. No, sir!

She'd been sold off in 1914, so someone must have been thinking – or not, as the case might be.

The ship he commanded was a B class destroyer, built in 1930, displacing 1,360 tons. She was, in Mitchell's judgement, the type of destroyer that represented most perfectly what was meant by the destroyer ideal. Oh, yes, the Tribals were heftier and far more rakish looking; but, somehow, the proportions of the destroyer classes from A to I seemed to him to be supreme.

They'd taken away his after 4.7" and the after bank of torpedo tubes and greatly augmented his outfit of depth charges. He welcomed every single depth charge that could be crammed aboard. He'd tried sinking U-boats with penny packets of charges, five dropped in the regulation pattern, and the scheme just didn't work.

You would, Dick Mitchell knew with a dark knowledge of events still to come, you would need one hell of a lot of depth charges to sink one lousy U-boat.

He had seventy. That was not enough. Even the old V&W's rebuilt as long range escorts had a hundred and ten.

But with what he had and with growing skill painfully acquired over the months of heartbreaking escort duty he would go out and damn well sink U-boats. That, as far as he was concerned, was what this war was all about.

'We rendezvous with *Pathan*, and Captain Elliot.' Mitchell shouldered his way out of the chartroom and back towards his bridge. He did not like to be off the bridge for any length of time when there was a war on. 'On this course – we'll run on to the beach in the States, I shouldn't wonder.'

Andy Stevens nodded and continued to look respectfully knowing.

'Straggler –' he started to say.

Mitchell stood looking out with the breeze on his face, odd flecks of high-driven spray stinging over him. 'With a Tribal?'

'Well –'

The Engine Room voicepipe emitted a sound like water running out of a plughole coupled with a lunatic banging of sledgehammers on corrugated-iron fences. The noise shocked into Mitchell's brain. Each segment of the uproar was tied in with some enormous calamity in the engine-room.

When the Chief reported, the damage was not quite as

bad as Mitchell could have expected; but it was bad enough.

'How long, Chief?'

That, always, was the question.

The Chief's voice up the pipe sounded thin and detached, the voice of a man who was weighing his words.

'It'll need three hours—'

'Make it two—'

'Give me two and a half—'

'That's all I can give you. *Pathan* will be—you can guess.'

'Aye.'

Bruiser wallowed, the way coming off her and the sea taking her into its cruel embrace. Hardened stomachs used to the swift cut and surge of the destroyer would heave up with this new queasy, empty motion.

Mitchell shoved himself deeper into his chair on the bridge and bent his head, and composed himself.

If a U-boat showed up now—good bye *Bruiser*.

Oberleutnant z. S. Baldur Wolz had to compose his own thoughts into patterns that conduced to sanity. Here he was, a U-boat commander, with the war at sea demanding every U-boat and every effort from U-boat personnel, stuck on a ship that orbited a rendezvous point waiting for something. The world was racketing away and he was not a part of it. It was funny, and also it was too deadly serious to be anything other than funny. Those idiot English with whom he had spent a few rowdy times would see the funny side, right enough.

Dick Mitchell, a few years older, was a right madman when it came to pranks. Wolz standing his watch in *Kiruna* felt a quick and treacherous stab of affection for those old days before the war. If Mitchell and he confronted each other now their mutual duties would be to kill the other.

Insane!

And yet – if only the stupid English would see the war was lost and surrender gracefully. Then – why then some of the dark forebodings Wolz had sensed in his conversations with people higher in the hierarchy than he, when they came about, would be that much lighter and easier to bear.

There had been easy pickings out in the Atlantic last year. Because U-55 had been in such bad shape after her exploits Wolz had been deprived of much of the success he might have enjoyed. He'd been temporarily attached to a training flotilla up in the Baltic and had bellowed and raved at the new men to knock them into shape. A difference was apparent in Germany these days. He had already remarked it. Regulations still held everyone in thrall; and because as a naval officer he had been spared much of officialdom, the changing conditions surprised him. But he was still navy, still cocooned within the navy framework, and he was dedicated to the U-boats. If he missed a very great deal of what was going on, he merely shared that with his fellow officers.

No one had done brilliantly well during the winter.

The British must have re-routed the convoys, and Donitz sent his boats out to seek them. The pickings remained lean, and Wolz's trip in which he had picked up just one target and one success was typical. But, with the Spring!

Willi Weidmann, an old comrade from U-42, came down to the schloss for a visit.

Willi seemed the same as ever, a thin, elegant young man with a wild streak in him that all the U-boat service in the world could not, it appeared, subdue.

'And, Baldur! If I shine the commandant's shoes for him and kiss his bald head –'

'You'll get a boat?'

'Yes!'

'Congratulations. But, Willi – are you sure you know one end of a boat from the other?'

Willi didn't look hurt.

'You think I'm – ' he began, and then Gertrude walked through the door out on to the terrace. She wore a fur coat pulled up about her ears and her face shone. She was the one with the mole beside her nose. She sparkled at them as they rose politely.

'Come inside, you two!' she commanded. 'It's cold enough out here to –'.

'Young ladies do not express themselves in that fashion!'

Gertrude laughed and pushed the door open, backing away, into the warmth of the schloss.

'If we are all to die, you stick-in-the-muds, then –'

'Who says we are all to die?' demanded Wolz, rather more sharply than he intended.

Willi was about to say something in his elegant squeak. He stopped. He shut his jaw. His protuberant eyes goggled.

Gertrude, her hair shining in the lamps, slowly opened the front of the fur coat.

She wore a brassiere that was pushed down under her breasts, a strip of black lace. She wore black stockings, and high-heeled shoes. The fur coat shadowed the pinkness of her flesh.

'We are ready to play again and I'm in a hurry!' she called.

Willi licked his lips.

Wolz thought of Marlene and her shocking SS uniform. He sighed. Germany had really won the war. So why were these people – who were in touch with other people who knew far more about what was going on – taking this *Gotterdammerüng* attitude?

Gertrude, for instance, who might only be a private secretary, must be in the position to know a great deal. She would say nothing, of course. Willi, like Wolz himself, could only guess. But the air of tenseness and of fatalism pervaded everyone with any insights.

Wolz itched to get back to his U-boat.

The next cruise, he knew, would be a good one.

'Come on!' And Gertrude switched the fur coat closed over the revealed loveliness. They followed her into the schloss. The game, this night, was sharper than ever.

But Wolz, thinking of Trudi, thinking of Lisl, had to force himself to look with leering pleasure on Gertrude, and to make himself take Mariza's half-nude body into his arms and dance to the gramophone.

Her breath fluttered warm on his cheek.

'Baldur! You aren't here!'

He could feel her, the softness of her flesh under his fingers, the hard ridge of her spine, the swell of her buttocks. She moved with him nicely as they danced. The gramophone jangled.

'Of course I am!'

'No.' She drew her head back to stare up at him.

'No. I think you are somewhere else.'

'And where would that be?'

She laughed again. All the mousiness left her in these moments when she used the excuse of the silly game and could throw off inhibition with her clothes. Wolz could feel her, all right, warm against him, her touch forcing his attention.

'Where? If it isn't one of two places I'll – I'll –'

'Yes?'

'If you aren't thinking of your U-boat or a woman then I'm wrong.'

'And if it was a woman?'

She pouted, and pressed herself closely to him, gripping him, unashamed. They had been drinking. Her hair swirled.

'I'd be jealous.'

'Then it was the U-boat.'

'I'm still jealous!'

He made himself pull her in even closer so her breasts squashed against his chest. He stroked her back. He looked into her eyes. Suddenly, he realised that he was not prepared to abandon tonight for dreams. He would lie, and lie joyfully.

71

'I was,' he said, bending his head to her and whispering in her ear, 'wondering which way –'

'Baldur!'

'Let's get out of here.'

'But – the others – this is a party –'

'Look at Willi and Gertrude.'

The other party-goers, all in various stages of undress, laughing and giggling and variously asking silly questions or dancing there and then, became aware of Willi and Gertrude.

Mariza sucked in her breath.

'I really think –'

'To dance just like that,' said Wolz, 'demands a certain skill. Luckily they are of a height to suit.'

'Yes, but!'

'I think, Mariza, if you do not come away right here and now I shall show you how to dance like that.'

'You . . . You would!'

'I would.'

She stopped dancing and half-turned away, her face flushed.

She did, Wolz reminded himself gravely, look remarkably lovely.

'Very well – Baldur . . .'

So out they went, laughingly joking with the others, passing Willi who was dancing in a kind of drunken stupor, his eyes fast shut, his mouth stretched, a gleeful look of complete absorption on his cheerful face.

Gertrude's face, slick with sweat, regarded them with blank, drugged eyes as she danced. Her mouth was wide open, soft and moist, and she panted.

Wolz sighed.

Willi would need all the memories he could cram into that scatter-brained skull of his when he was out on patrol.

They went through into Uncle Siegfried's study. The swastika, the bronze busts, the shelved books, frowned down. A single lamp burned in a corner. The massive

72

safe glistened opposite. Wolz didn't even bother to look. He slid his arms around Mariza and pulled her close and kissed her.

When they broke apart, she panted and put a hand to her hair.

'You –'

'Yes.'

'But this is the study where –'

'You have worked here for my uncle, Mariza. Now it is my turn. Of course, the nature of the work is different.'

She giggled.

As he stroked her bare back, she said: 'Do you have a key to the safe, Baldur?'

'No. Never have. Why do you ask?'

'Oh, nothing. I just wondered.' She ran her fingers down his spine and he gasped. 'The others all do –'

'Yes. Well they are uncle's sons. I'm only a nephew.'

'Will they be back from leave soon?'

'I've no idea.' He eased her towards the upholstered sofa in the corner, the same sofa that both Lottie and Heidi could vouch for as a comfortable love-couch. 'Who the hell cares about them now?'

'Yes, yes, of course –'

She sank back on the sofa and drew him down towards her.

Wolz banished all nonsense about safes from his head. This was what mattered. This was what would sustain him when the icy spray slashed into his face on the bridge of U-55, when the depth-charges rained down, when the damned English tried to kill him. One thing was sure, the English couldn't take *this* away from him . . .

By the time he reported back for duty Wolz fancied he knew quite a fair amount about Mariza Kalman. Despite that he was vaguely aware that she kept much of herself to herself, not sharing her deeper thoughts with him. He respected this. He most certainly had not shared his own dreams of Lisl and Trudi with her, and he suspected there had been a man in her life who had let her down, betrayed her, been the smirking seducing villain beloved of fiction. That was not Wolz's business.

The winter had been foul and rain slashed down as Wolz returned. He turned up the collar of his coat and stepped determinedly into the downpour.

As he felt he must do, he kept a weather eye open just in case that blot Adolf Forstner had sent some more bully boys along to beat him up. The last time Forstner himself had been with them, and had, no doubt, regretted that fact.

But Wolz saw nothing to alarm him as he made his way along the jetty to U-55. Sentries prowled, their steel helmets gleaming in the rain. The U-boat looked thin and ghost like in the slanting lances of rain, and the sea surface leaped with little white spouts, miniature watery volcanoes.

The saddle tanks which gave the boat so much breadth and apparent solidity were awash, and the deck gratings glittered, the water tumbling and splintering. The flag drooped. The watch spotted him in time so that he was received with due ceremony, and he paused for a few low-spoken words with the First Lieutenant.

'Well, Kern. All ship-shape?'

'All ready, skipper. Except Schmidt is missing.'

Wolz frowned.

Machinist's Mate Schmidt, if he missed the patrol, would be very sorry for himself. The Kriegsmarine would see to that.

'Well, we have our orders. If he's not joined by the time we sail then he knows what he's in for. D'you know of any new trouble at home?'

'No, sir. His wife was expecting – but that's all.'

'I expect that's it, then. The fool. He's only himself to blame. Wait until the very last moment, Kern, and then put in a report. Give him all the rope we can.'

'To hang himself, most likely.'

'Yes.'

The Chief, Leutnant Kurt Loeffler, appeared and gave his opinion that if the Ark had been built by the men who had serviced U-55 then the human race would have perished.

'But we'll swim long enough, skipper.'

'Long enough to sink tonnage?'

'Yes. But if we take too much of a pounding I'll not answer for the boat. And, skipper, I mean it.'

Wolz frowned.

The truth was, U-55 had taken a beating. She was on her last legs. But until the new boats that were building came forward then U-boat officers like Wolz must continue to fight the war at sea with what there was available.

Again he felt gratitude that he had an engineer officer like Loeffler. If the boat's L.I. – the Leitender Ingenieur, the Chief Engineer – was not absolutely on top of his job then everyone was in trouble.

Reports from the other departments were correct. The boat was ready for sea. The trim dive had been successfully completed, stores were aboard, carefully packed so that those required first were stowed last. The sausages swung like red and black bloated stalactites. Spare torpedoes were stowed. The ammunition lockers were full. Everything was ready.

There was nothing to stop U-55 from going to sea.

Nothing except the English.

Baldur Wolz had no intention of letting them stop him, none whatsoever . . .

CHAPTER SEVEN

U-55 nosed into the scud of the North Atlantic. The grey day was almost done. The weather remained foul. That did not worry Wolz. In bad weather the convoys lost touch and individual ships found great difficulty in maintaining station in the once orderly files. Then there were likely to be stragglers.

U-boats welcomed stragglers.

Wolz's orders called for him to join a patrol line to the south of Iceland. Der Löwe, as Karl Donitz, B.d.U., was sometimes called, had come to the conclusion that the English must be routing their convoys far to the northwards. That would explain the thin pickings of the winter. Some convoys had been caught and execution wrought.

And, too, *Scharnhorst* and *Gneisenau* had been out and chalked up a notable success sailing back in triumph. Instead of returning to Germany they had put in at Brest. Soon, the general opinion in the Kriegsmarine had it, they would put to sea again with *Bismarck*. With a heavy cruiser by them, perhaps two if they could be got ready in time, *Hipper* and *Prince Eugen*, the surface fleet would go out and carve such huge slices from the fat English merchant shipping that the war could be won in a week.

That, Wolz knew, was the fervent hope of the surface ship men of the navy.

He continued to sail U-55 in search of the convoys. He harboured his own doubts; and he did not discuss them with anyone at all.

The patrol line ought to sweep up a convoy. Less than

a week ago Prien in U-47 had spotted a convoy and attacks had taken place. Wolz had picked up the reports flowing over the air.

Nothing much was heard after that, and Headquarters had been calling U-47 and U-70 on and off without obtaining any replies.

Well, there were many reasons why a U-boat did not reply to calls.

Wolz could not believe that the Bull of Scapa had been sunk. That just did not seem possible.

When a sighting report came in from Lemp in U-110 an electric current seemed to flicker through the boat.

'Well within range, skipper,' said Ehrenberger, delighted, rubbing his hands.

'Agreed. Chief, give us all you've got. If we make full revolutions we can be up with the sighting by nightfall.'

'Full revolutions,' said Loeffler. 'I'll give you full revolutions. I just hope the screws don't fall off.'

But all the Chief's gloomy prognostications could not cut the air of anticipation. This time, the men of U-55 knew they were going in for the kill.

Up here near Iceland the weather was seldom kind and at this time of the year could be expected to produce freakish conditions of extreme difficulty. It was up to Wolz to make full use of every climatic condition he could.

The rumble of the twin diesels shook the boat. The grey water scythed away from her bows and ran creaming and foaming along her saddle tanks. The wind cut cruelly at the men on the exposed bridge.

Wolz stared ahead. His lookouts kept their eyes fixed firmly on their quadrants. The feel of his command shuddering through the seas, the lift and sway and lurch of her, the sea smashing away from the sharp bows, all these physical sensations combined to bring an exultant sense of once again being on the hunt, once more hurtling forward into action.

U-55 crashed through the seas, anxious to get in among

the English freighters and tankers.

By the time Lemp's report had been digested by B.d.U. and the expected orders to the boats in the area to form a wolfpack had been sent out, U-55 was well on the way. Lemp had attacked and had sunk a ten thousand ton tanker.

'Just let us get at them!' said Ehrenberger.

'There will be some left for us, Kern.'

Ehrenberger laughed, his bearded face shining in the lights of the control room. 'I tend to doubt it, skipper – Kretschmer and Schepke are in the picture, you know.'

'I know.'

If Prien was gone – and that was unthinkable – the two leading aces were Kretschmer in U-99 and Schepke in U-100.

Baldur Wolz had a fair bit of leeway to make up to catch them.

Long before they spotted the ships of the convoy they were aware exactly of its position in the vastness of the ocean.

Away on the northern horizon flames broke up.

A glowing ball rose into the blackness, expanding, shining, refulgent. The orange glare spread over the sky, enormous, shooting up soundlessly. What seemed a long time later the boom of that tremendous explosion reached them.

'Come on Chief!' said Wolz. But he spoke to himself.

He stood on his bridge, his feet braced, that black cheroot jammed into the corner of his mouth and slanting arrogantly upwards, his fierce predatory face gazing hungrily over the curve of the ocean towards action.

The ships of the convoy furrowed their painful way from Canada to England, and in the seas around them swarmed the U-boats of the wolf pack. A brotherhood of arms, the men of the U-boats, each crew isolated in it own steel cocoon and yet all bound together by th commands of B.d.U. and their mutual dedication to th struggle. The aces were there, and the men taking ou their boats for the first time. They prowled through the water, hidden by night and weather, and they rent and tore the flanks of the convoy, burning and sinking. This was war, and it was not pretty, and it made a man either rise above it or sink into gibbering idiocy beneath the horror of it all.

Wolz had seen both reactions in his time.

The battle on the horizon neared as U-55 plunged on. Visibility was reasonable, enough so that the lookouts in the English ships would have the greatest difficulty in spotting the tiny shape of a U-boat's conning tower in the grey waste, whilst the men of the U-boat pack could see the lumbering freighters with stark clarity.

The torpedo aimer with the binoculars already in position abaft the sky periscope waited for Wolz. The hatch was open and the attack periscope abaft that was sunk in its well. Wolz gripped the coaming of the wind deflector and peered ahead. Spray hit the deflector halfway up the tower and burst brilliantly away. U-55 surged on, quartering the wind.

If the English lookouts in the big freighters, high up, could not see the conning tower of a boat, the lookouts in the destroyers had a better chance.

Not a much better chance, but a little better.

Wolz spotted the twin white bow waves, curving away like wings, cutting through the dark sea. His fingers gripped harder.

'Destroyer –' came the yell of the lookout.

It was Hans Loos. Wolz would have a word with him later about the tardiness of his warning.

Now everyone in the boat held their breaths waiting for the skipper to order the expected dive.

Wolz stared fixedly at the onrushing destroyer.

She would pass fifteen hundred metres at least.

He said nothing.

U-55 slogged on.

He heard Ehrenberger's cough from the tower float up.

His face like granite, Wolz held on.

The destroyer swerved across their path, racing through the sea, haring for the stern of the convoy. She was a destroyer, a V & W class, with a cutdown aft smokestack. She looked lean and powerful, smothered in spray, forcing her way on. Moments later a blast of fire reached into the heavens from the starboard column. One of the rear markers had been torpedoed.

The destroyer swirled away and vanished in the murk.

'Close.' Ehrenberger's voice floated up.

'If we'd dived, he'd have picked us up on his listening devices. They can't see us on the surface. They don't have a chance.'

'Sooner them than us.'

'And someone is hard at work back there. I'm taking us in from the tail of the convoy, also, Kern.'

'You're going right in, skipper?'

If there was hesitation in Wolz's reply it was lost in the smash of the waves and the rumble of the diesels.

'Yes.'

'We're ready down here –'

'If you run into any difficulties I'll loose from up here.'

'Very good!'

What Wolz was intending to do was tricky. But it was an accepted part of the attack techniques of daring U-boat commanders and whilst Wolz had no wish to be daring to foolhardiness he had absolute confidence in himself and his men, and almost absolute confidence in his boat. Faithful old U-55 had been driven hard and if she was to play up, no one could really blame her. Wolz just prayed she wouldn't do something awkward right in the middle of the convoy.

A succession of dark blotches against the night, the ships of the convoy moved ponderously towards the east. They moved from port to starboard as viewed from L-55. Two more ships blossomed into fire, and there were others who died more quietly. But the size of the convoy gave Wolz no misgivings that his fellow U-boatmen would have destroyed it all before he got there.

Flames danced across the water, filling shadowy hollows with orange light. Against the inferno of a dying ship a lifeboat drifted. A few black silhouettes showed as men attempted to bring order to the chaos that enveloped them. U-55 ghosted past and the shipwrecked seamen were too engrossed in dealing with their injured and organising oarsmen to pull out of the path of the burning ship to notice the sleek and deadly shape of the U-boat.

Farther on half of a ship drifted, upended, the shambles on the deck dripping coils of rope and wires, wreckage, smashed crates, parts of aeroplanes, splintered lifeboats. The halfship wallowed past, deserted and forlorn. Wolz could see no sign of life.

His boat eased on to the stern of the convoy.

'Starboard ten.'

'Starboard ten.'

If a prowling destroyer spotted them now . . .

The V & W they had seen was nowhere in sight, she'd probably gone haring back up the port side of the convoy. Now Wolz steered U-55 directly on the track of the convoy. The ships lumbered along ahead of him. The lookouts were fully aware of the gambit their skipper was making, and they strained their eyes into the flame-shot darkness.

If the U-boat was caught silhouetted against the flames, and the destroyer raced in . . .

Through the water the distant rumble of depth charges indicated a destroyer thought she was in contact with a submerged U-boat. Wolz frowned. If a comrade had been caught below the surface it was almost a sure thing he had been forced to dive.

U-55 ran on. Now she was up with the rearmost ships. Wolz peered ahead. He was between the fifth and sixth columns. A tanker showed just ahead. Wolz took a careful sweep around, seeing the lurching ships moving solidly on, the flames masked by the outlines of a big three island freighter, the glitter on the water, a worry-ing hint of betraying phosphorous at his own bows. He could see no destroyers.

'Starboard,' he called down to the obersteuermann in the tower. 'Check. Hold it . . .' His mind performed the calculations. The attack table below would be chunking out the figures and Ehrenberger at the attack periscope would be –

'I've got him, skipper. All lined up.'

'When you're ready – and, Kern – don't miss!'

'Not this close, skipper!'

U-55 gave a lurching wiggle at that moment, writhing in the sea, and spray slashed inboard. The water sliced across Wolz's face. He did not move.

When he could see again he took the black cheroot from his mouth and tossed it overboard.

'Hold her on, Kern!'

Over there the freighters lumbered on. The tanker showed as big as a block of flats. The gun on her stern was lashed fore and aft. She rolled heavily in the sea.

Beyond her in the next column a small freighter showed as a black bar extension of the tanker's stern. U-55 lay athwart the convoy. Her four forward tubes bore down on the flank from inside the box of ships.

'Loose!'

The thud of the departing torpedo, the hiss of com-pressed air, the surge of the boat . . .

Hungrily, Wolz stared forward.

'Loose!'

The bosun in the control room would be counting now. Everyone would be counting under their breath.

Wolz brought U-55 around, smoothly, once more paralleling the course of the convoy. He let her head pay off, swinging around to port, ready to let his re-maining two torpedoes loose on the port flank.

'Eels running!'

They waited.

Wolz waited with half his mind. The other half

watched the silhouettes of the ships as they swung around from left to right, coming on to a bows-on position. He bent to give the order and the tanker split apart.

The fireball spat into the sky. The lurid violence of the flame and the concussion drove him back, blustering wind scorching past his face. He felt the blast of heat.

The tanker disintegrated.

'My God!' someone yelled.

'Take the freighter ahead, Kern! Good shooting!'

Another explosion blasted from the darkness as the ship beyond the tanker took a torpedo in her guts.

'Two gone!'

'Loose!'

'Loose!'

Two more torpedoes sped from U-55's tubes.

'Stern tube stand by!'

U-55 continued to swing to port.

Wolz performed the mental gymnastics to align himself with the stern tube.

The ship he picked looked to be a useful size – it was not quite a case of picking and choosing despite the number of targets.

He'd have to let U-55 swing to port just a fraction more to bring the stern tube on, and when he had loosed bring her back for a straight run out of the tail of the convoy.

He waited and the second pair of eels struck.

Two ships blew apart – and then Wolz frowned.

A third explosion had ripped into the concussions and he saw quite clearly a second spout of white water against the side of the nearer ship.

'Someone else put an eel into her!'

'Yes,' said Wolz. 'Keep your eyes skinned.'

The stern tube was on . . .

'Loose!'

'Destroyer!'

Wolz whirled. He gripped the coaming and peered off to the starboard quarter. A destroyer was cutting through aft of the sinking freighter, her upperworks and funnel illuminated in a ghastly orange glare from the burning tanker.

As he stared his mind raced like the attack table itself over angles and chances. Stupid to dive. He had to keep on moving on the surface – the ship out there was small and single funnelled and although he, like his comrades, would call her a destroyer, she was not a real destroyer. She didn't have the lines. She was altogether too tubby and small. She was foaming along and lurching into the sea and yet Wolz estimated her speed as being an optical illusion.

'Chief! Give us everything!'

U-55 kicked ahead, surging at her best speed through the water, diesels thundering, roaring away.

'Eel!'

Again Wolz whirled to the quadrant from which the lookout screamed his warning.

The glimmering track of a torpedo showed. The streak arrowed for the side of U-55.

The confusion of the night, the noise and the fires, the smash of the sea, all faded as Wolz stared in sick apprehension at that deadly onrushing streak.

Death foamed towards them.

Death loosed from the tubes of a comrade!

'Stop starboard. Full ahead port. Come on! Come on!'

With her wheel hard over and her starboard engine stopped and her screw thrusting her stern around, U-55 pirouetted in the sea.

Rockets burst from the torpedoed ships, and the lurid glares of fires lit the sky.

Wolz stared at the torpedo as it raced in.

U-55 swung.

The destroyer that was not a destroyer pounded on and away into the shadows. Reflections of the flames danced over the water. The torpedo scuttered along just beneath the surface. It creamed past U-55's stern. It went roiling away and on into the confusion.

Wolz let out his breath.

'Half speed on both.'

U-55 straightened up. She withdrew from the convoy, at a speed at which her bow wave would not betray her. There were destroyers with the convoy, and they meant business. Once again the distant thud of depth charges echoed through the water.

'We got them,' said Ehrenberger. His voice was curiously flat. 'Five, was it, skipper?'

'One at least was shared. Possibly two. I wonder who that was, shooting at our birds?'

'Whoever he was, he's in trouble.'

'Yes. Reload all tubes. There might be chance for another shoot tonight.'

Wolz doubted that.

He would pace the convoy from a safe distance astern. But there had been an aggressiveness about the escorts he hadn't experienced before. They had failed to spot him; but they had come very close.

The night remained dark and close, and the convoy drew away to a safe distance before Wolz decided to alter course. The flames were dying down. There were men in the water over there, burned men, boiled men, dying men. That was the fortune of war. He could do nothing for them.

Reaction was hitting him now. He must not let it interfere with what he must do as the commander. His men must never be allowed to see any chink in his armour, any suggestion that he was less than a superman. Ludicrous though the idea was, it was absolutely necessary. By this time they had an absolute faith in him, sharing the conviction that if Baldur Wolz did a thing then that thing was right and would come out perfectly. There could be no letting up, not until the last eel had been loosed, not until they were safely moored up in Lorient.

'Destroyer!'

'Destroyer dead ahead!'

Wolz stared.

Yes – two destroyers! Two English bloodhounds sniffing around ready to rend him into pieces!

He looked again.

The dark shadows that were the English ships looked odd. One seemed to be stopped. The other was moving purposefully in a circle about the first. Stopped for engine trouble? Quite likely – that or a torpedo . . .

'Stop diesels. Quarter on electric motors. Silent discipline.'

The rumble of the diesels chuntered to silence and the unheard thrilling vibration of the electric motors began as the Chief grouped in. U-55 slid quietly across the sea.

'Starboard ten.'

'Starboard ten.'

On this new course they should pass well clear of the two destroyers. To dive now would invite disaster. Wolz looked again carefully at the two destroyers. They were V & W's. The stopped ship looked forlorn and vulnerable. Well, U-55's tubes were empty . . .

If the reloading could be done in record time, perhaps . . .

'U-boat, red twenty!'

Yes, over there, another U-boat, ghosting along.

Wolz surmised she had expended her eels and, like himself was reloading. Or she could have loosed her entire outfit and be empty. She slid along, heading for the two destroyers like a lean grey wolf. Surely she could see them?

Suddenly white water spouted alongside the U-boat. She started to dive. By the way she went down Wolz knew she had crash-dived, and he shook his head, surprised, wondering what had caused that. The two destroyers were clearly concerned about their own business and had never even suspected the presence of a surfaced U-boat near them.

The circling destroyer straightened up on her orbit. She picked up speed. Wolz refused to dive. He let U-55 creep off into the night, travelling slowly so that no betraying bow-wave could show him to the enemy look-outs.

The destroyer picked up speed. She was not going at her full rate of knots. She passed over the spot where the U-boat had dived.

Moments later the night was rent asunder by the explosion of depth charges and the sea boiled and spurted into white volcanoes in her wake.

Backwards and forwards she went.

Wolz watched, using his night glasses, almost at the limit of vision. He watched with sick fascination.

A comrade was down there, his boat being hammered and pummelled. The wabos, the wasserbomben, were raining down about that unknown U-boat. The depth-charges were blowing her lights out, shattering her gauges, sending smashing shocks through her hull, springing rivets.

'Come on, come on!' said Wolz. The glasses thrust against his eyes, stingingly. His hands were gripped into claws.

But the destroyer dropped another pattern of charges. The water boiled and broke and spouted white in the darkness.

Then –

'There he is!' bellowed a lookout.

But Wolz could see.

The U-boat broke surface, water spilling from her. She wallowed. Men appeared on her bridge. She was sinking. The destroyer nosed in. Just before that tableau vanished Wolz saw the way of it, what was going on, and he dragged the glasses from his eyes and smashed a fist against the bridge coaming.

'They got her!'

'At least they're not killed. The English are taking them prisoner!'

'Yes.'

When the tubes were reloaded, Wolz turned U-55 on to the track of the convoy. He had kept in touch by the

87

glare of fires in the sky. He felt forward cautiously, looking for the two destroyers. If he could put an eel into that stopped ship it would slow the English down . . .

He did not see the destroyers.

And by the time he had worked into a position from which to launch an attack the thin daylight had come and he had to turn away, and promise himself the attack for the next night.

He was daring when he had to be. He was not foolhardy. And getting his boat sunk and his men and himself killed would not help their comrades who had been taken prisoner, not an iota.

So they ran on the next day, waiting.

Most of a U-boatman's life consisted of waiting — waiting to go on patrol, waiting out the long hours of watch duty on the bridge or in the engine rooms, waiting out the patient stalking of a convoy, and then the waiting as the eels ran. A U-boatman knew how to wait.

Signals from B.d.U. were run through the Enigma coding machine and the results made Wolz screw up his lips.

His orders were to shadow the convoy and report position and course, all the usual fashion. He was to await further U-boats who were being hurried to the scene of the action as fast as Donitz could summon them and their commanders could drive them.

Down in the wardroom as U-55 ran on comfortably, they worked out the tonnages.

'The tanker was eight thousand,' said Wolz, stabbing the silhouette book.

'And the first freighter, the one beyond the tanker, was a good five thousand.' Ehrenberger looked challengingly at Wolz.

Wolz shook his head.

'She was three thousand five hundred. Here –' He riffled pages. 'There. Useless to claim any more.'

'All right. So what do we have?'

The tanker and the four freighters added up to a minimum of twenty five thousand five hundred G.R.T.

'Well,' Ehrenberger puffed out his cheeks.

Leutnant Freyer was on watch. Ludwig Riepold, the second, said: 'I'd have put it at more than that, skipper.'

'And don't forget, at least one and possibly two of these ships must be shared.'

'If it was the share of the boat we saw –' began Riepold. His face looked savage. 'Let's put Hellmuth's *Prelude* to Act Three on. At least, that way –'

'Quite,' said Wolz.

They looked at him.

When Daddy got that look on his face, his crew knew when to shut up.

Presently, Wolz stood up and shucked on his oilskins.

'I shall be on the bridge. You may play Hellmuth's record, if you wish. I'll thank you to keep the volume turned down.'

'Very good!'

As he climbed the ladder through the conning tower, Wolz wondered just who it was who had been sunk and captured.

Whoever it was, the war was over for him.

The war went on for U-55, and for Baldur Wolz.

CHAPTER EIGHT

As he rotted away in SS *Kiruna* Wolz's thoughts turned again and again to the details of his last patrol and the loss of the U-boat. The sinking and capture of the crew which he had witnessed had impressed him profoundly. With empty tubes he had been unable to attack, and at least the destroyer had picked up the U-boat's crew and had not left them to die. Wolz would have gone in and picked them up, of course, had the Englishmen not been there first.

As he paced *Kiruna's* bridge and fretted over his inactivity and tried to be polite to the officers, he recalled the sense of doom pervading the messages from B.d.U.

B.d.U. looked after the U-boats. They felt that personal sense of direction, of care, and obeyed their orders.

But as day followed day and the calls went unanswered, the conclusion appeared inescapable.

As U-47 and U-70 did not answer, so now U-99 and U-100 failed to respond to their callsigns.

It was all so damned depressing.

Schepke and Kretschmer – both gone?

It did not seem possible.

Three of the top aces, vanished, gone, lost, sunk – dead . . .

There had been rumours aplenty. But Donitz had issued no communiqués and nothing definite was known. What was known by the men of the U-boat flotillas was that Kretschmer, Schepke and Prien were no longer around

Donitz had reacted to something up there in the water off Iceland, for he had ordered his boats southward once more. U-55 had developed more trouble and it had been a dicy business getting her back to Lorient. Had Loeffle been less of a Chief than he was, U-55 would not have made it.

They'd had to dive for hostile aircraft and Wolz had been in such a hurry he'd got a thorough soaking. After that he'd developed a sniffle, and the sniffle went around the boat, and everyone was wet and miserable and every nose was like a port navigation light.

Schmidt's absence meant that one man was always just that much overburdened. When men were lost through casualties, the remainder somehow didn't seem to mind so much about extra duty. But when it was because a man had failed to join the ship the atmosphere was far different. Schmidt was in for a whole lot of trouble, that was for sure.

They had a chance at a runner, a ship slugging on alone across the hostile sea.

The attack was carried out in meticulous fashion; but – and no satisfactory reason could be discovered – two torpedoes missed. Before the third could be loosed a damned destroyer appeared sniffing about and U-55 broke off the action.

The ease with which Baldur Wolz eluded the English destroyer and got clear away meant, in the eyes of his crew, that he was this superman, this Sea Wolf, this master at the art of underwater warfare. To Wolz himself it meant only that he knew a few tricks, that the Englishman did not know as much, and that he'd been lucky.

Very lucky.

They tried a shot at the destroyer; but she eluded the eels and that left them with the singleton in the stern tube.

Wolz had had trouble before in getting rid of a single torpedo, and he was likely to have more. But he disliked the idea of returning to base with an eel still in his tubes. B.d.U. on receipt of his report made no bones of the matter.

U-55 was ordered to proceed to Lorient, no argument.

So it was a Baldur Wolz who felt that what had begun with so much promise had ended in anticlimax, who sailed his command back to base.

As they followed the minesweeper up the swept channel they were bombed. The English bombers roared in, casting their eggs upon the shore installations and the ships. Wolz simply submerged and let the Luftwaffe flak gunners and the English fight it out. That was their war. His was in abeyance for a space. The moment the yards got U-55 to rights he'd be off again, ready to fight his own war once more.

When he ordered the tanks to be blown to surface, the vertical main ballast pump coughed twice and then refused to function. Loeffler went raging past, his face inflamed, an enormous spanner in his grease-stained hand.

Wolz sighed.

U-55 was falling to pieces around his ears.

Wolz went through the circular pressurised door, ducking his head, and straightened to a crouch beside Loeffler. The control wheels and valves, the piping, the pumps and the noisy breathing of the Chief made a symphony of effort well in keeping with Freyer's Lohengrin.

'You're having trouble, Chief?'

'Trouble?' The Chief hefted his spanner as though he would strike the big pump.

'Muck. That's what it is. We come all this way and we get French muck in the pump. It'll take me—'

'As soon as you can, I know. I'll go along to the wardroom and have some black sweat while you're working I'll put something in it, too. If there's any left.'

'Leave some for me, skipper!' called Loeffler as Wolz ducked back through the round doorway.

The pump was fixed and wheezed and groaned and the water somehow was forced out of the ballast tanks U-55 lolloped to the surface and the worried skipper o the minesweeper blinked a reproachful message at them

'Pity you couldn't join us,' Wolz morsed back.

So that was how U-55 returned to base after that patrol.

When Wolz's relief came up to *Kiruna's* bridge to take over the watch, Wolz yawned and passed a few words handing over, then he clattered down the metal rungs of the companionway treads to see about a late meal. They ate well aboard, that was one fact he couldn't argue about. Also, he wanted one of his cigars.

Kapitän Miehle met him, half-smiling.

'You will be pleased to learn, Herr Oberleutnant, that a U-boat is expected. You are to return in her.'

Wolz's sharp-featured, square-cut face betrayed not a flicker of emotion. His blond hair slicked in the overhead lighting.

'Thank you, Herr Kapitän. I am very pleased to hear it.'

Miehle looked at him askance.

'Odd signal. U-boat was mentioned – U-112 – but not the name of the commander. ETA eleven hundred tomorrow.'

'U-112? No – I've no idea who commands. She was not out of Lorient, not my flotilla.'

'You U-boat chaps keep things close to your chests.' Miehle allowed himself a smile. 'You'll be glad to be off my ship. I can guess. May I offer you a small drink before you turn in?'

'I was going for a meal – yes, Herr Kapitän, that is most thoughtful.'

They went through to Miehle's cabin and Wolz reflected that he missed the camaraderie of the Kommando room at base. Donitz set up the Kommando room so that captains of U-boats could have the opportunity to relax in comfort and swap stories and fill each other in about their experiences. Commanders of U-boats only. That was the rule. He'd spent a few pleasant hours there, talking shop, or not talking shop, getting away from it all. But the sense of comradeship was precious to a U-boatman particularly when he was isolated and alone in command, beneath the sea and the wabos were tumbling down about his ears.

Miehle wanted to talk about U-boats. He had no real conception of the underwater weapon or its uses. Wolz remained polite. But he was aware of his own distance, his own feelings of detachment. If you didn't slam the hatch on top of your head and shut yourself into the cocoon of the U-boat's intestinal machinery and dive down and down into the depths, then you just didn't know.

Wolz got the captain off U-boats after a bit and they talked about girls and some of the Berlin shows.

'Of course, Paris is the place. I remember –' Miehle screwed up his eyes. 'Well, there's the Pou Bleu. You must try it when you're next on leave in Paris. The Blue Flea will pin your eyelids back, I can tell you.'

'Thank you. If I'm in Paris –'

'If!'

'Headquarters are there and I usually report in on my way through.'

'Yes. I've heard Admiral Donitz has a personal relationship with his U-boat commanders.'

'That is so. He gets around a great deal, from base to base.'

'Well, Herr Oberleutnant, it will be the big ships who will win the war. And quickly. Once the thirty eight centimeters start shooting –'

He paused, checking himself.

Then he laughed and drained his glass.

'You said something about a meal?'

'Yes, Herr Kapitän. Thank you for the drink.' Wolz rose. He looked back. 'Whilst I am glad to be leaving *Kiruna*, I would like to express my appreciation of your hospitality.'

'Think nothing of it! We big ship men have a fondness for you U-boat maniacs. Goodnight!'

'Goodnight.'

HMS *Bruiser* picked up speed cautiously.

Dick Mitchell sat hunched on his bridge, muffled against the cold, feeling the tremble through the fabric of his command, willing the engines to keep turning, willing misfortune to go away and drown its damned self.

He bent to the voicepipe.

'What can you let me have, Chief?'

The answering rumble might have come from some drunken inferno.

'Aye, skipper, aye. I can give you revolutions for twenty knots. Mebbe three quarters over the top if you kick hard. But if –'

'All right. Well done.'

'Aye, oh, aye.'

'Who'd be an engineer?' said Andy Stevens. He essayed a small laugh. 'If it wasn't for string and chewing gum we'd never get moving.'

The old destroyer cut through the sea, and the Pilot came to report, not in too happy a frame of mind.

'Well, we'll just have to make the time up. *Pathan* will be full of wrath and fury. You know these top-line Fleet destroyer skippers.' Mitchell glanced at the sub. He was a fine mathematician. If he was kicked, as the Chief suggested, from time to time, it might help – or, shrewdly surmised Mitchell, knowing men, it might not. 'Do the best you can for us, Pilot.'

'Aye, aye, sir.'

With the dawn they ought to run on to the rendezvous and pick up *Pathan*. Then the show was in the hands of Elliot. What that show would be Mitchell would find out. Meantime he waited out the hours of the passage.

He stood up with a creak and started for the bridge ladder.

'I'll be in my cabin,' he said in the formula that was quite unnecessary and yet must be said. 'Call me the instant anything blows.'

'Aye, aye sir.'

What a way, he thought in some disgruntled amuse-

95

ment as he stretched out tiredly, what a way to run a war.

He was called when *Bruiser* picked up *Pathan*, and he climbed to the bridge and peered across the grey waters.

There were two ships out there.

Pathan, a Tribal class destroyer, was immediately visible. She looked long and low and lean with those raked funnels and the eight 4.7" in twin mountings. Her Aldiss lamp blinked furiously and the yeoman of signals was hard at it. Mitchell looked at her consort.

'That's *Kestrel*.'

'Two Fleet destroyers,' said Stevens, who came up on to the bridge then and peered over towards those lean grey shapes. 'Something's up.'

'We're hardly in their league. Well, yeoman?'

'Conform to my movements, sir.'

Mitchell grunted to himself. So Elliot of *Pathan* was giving nothing away. The Aldiss blinked again and gave *Bruiser* steaming stations. The three destroyers picked up speed and began to surge ahead. Mitchell frowned. If he made a signal saying his best speed was twenty knots he rather fancied old Elliot would have an apoplectic fit. Yet if these two hulking great Fleet destroyers, a Tribal and a K class, worked up to full revolutions he would be left a long long way astern. But there was no use in shillyshallying.

'Make a signal to *Pathan*,' he said. He spelt out the bad news.

The two ships from the Home Fleet would, of course, consider themselves far superior to a mere escort. But my Lords of the Admiralty must know what they were doing. Whatever was in the wind, *Bruiser* must do her best to play her part.

The lamp flickered like a will o' the wisp.

The yeoman's face was straight as he reported.

'Steer two three five. And try to keep up.'

'Acknowledge.'

Mitchell fumed.

White water kicked up from the sterns of his consorts. They began to move ahead.

In a flat sea *Pathan* could reach over 36.5 knots and *Kestrel* almost as much. He'd see them disappear over the horizon in no time.

'Steer two three five,' he said. Then, to the Chief, he said down the pipe: 'Give me what you can, Chief. They're hanging out a rope over their sterns.'

'Aye, so they might, skipper. But I'd like to get where we're going in one piece.'

What, said Mitchell to himself, what a bloody way to run a bloody war.

The sea ran in long grey swathes, with a stiff nor' westerly hinting at dirty weather to come. That was no news. The two big Fleet destroyers clearly considered that what was afoot could be handled by them, and by them alone. The old escort destroyer could make her best speed and arrive up when the action was all over.

That didn't suit Dick Mitchell.

Something big was due to happen. Somewhere over the horizon on this course, how far away he couldn't know, the balloon was due to go up.

He remembered old Elliot. A full Commander, he'd been blown up at Dunkirk and everyone said since then he had a tin ear. He would not take kindly to a Lieutenant Commander requesting additional information. *Bruiser* must simply pound on plugging away as fast as she could.

Mitchell had overheard a conversation, in a Plymouth bar, that had made him blazingly angry at the time.

A couple of RNVR lieutenants had been talking to a Royal Marine captain. They had been drinking, and were feeling not so much merry as free to express large opinions on the world, on Hitler and Churchill and on the navy in general.

' "Wavy Navy", they call us,' one of the lieutenants had said, and took a long plug of his beer. No pink gin for him.

The other hiccoughed, and, somewhat owlishly, said: 'The RN fellows look down their noses at us. Yet all they do is swan about in their damned great battlewagons. The real work in this war is being done by the escorts and the coastal boys. That's us. You tell a true-blue navy chap that, and see what he says.'

The marine had been judiciously sympathetic, and taken himself off with the blonde in the too-tight dress. The two Wavy Navy lieutenants had ordered more beer and moaned about the way the real navy – and that was a laugh – contumed the little ship men.

Well, as *Bruiser* struggled to keep going in the wake of those two snooty Fleet destroyers, all muscle and punch, Dick Mitchell, for all he was regular navy himself, understood just what those two Wavy Navy blokes had been getting on about.

He liked the way the shorter one had used the word 'contume'. It sounded odd, spluttered out around the foam from his pint. But it all added up.

The little ships of the escort forces were the boys to beat the U-boats, and that meant winning the war.

And *Bruiser* was not so little as all that, either. She still had three 4.7″ guns, and four 21″ torpedo tubes, and if it came to it, she'd go in alongside the Tribal and the K.

And with those thoughts Mitchell at last acknowledged to himself that what that something was over the horizon, it was likely to be pretty scarifying.

Secrets proliferated during the war at sea. He'd not failed to notice the new and odd-looking aerials in *Pathan*. Radio Location devices operating on land could give a very good idea of the co-ordinates of a ship at sea unwary enough to transmit messages. But that was on long range. Short waves were another matter. Mitchell, like all the escort commanders, was well aware of the U-boats' penchant for chattering over the air. Donitz liked to keep in touch with his boats. All this radio traffic was monitored. It was in code, of course, and to break the code was the dream of Naval Intelligence.

Mitchell knew only what a destroyer skipper would know of all that cloak and dagger stuff. But his standing orders included a strong injunction that, should the opportunity come his way, he was to capture any documents, ciphers, code books and machines he could. That was top priority.

As *Bruiser* ran on over the uneasy sea the watches changed and Mitchell did not leave his bridge. The two Fleet destroyers vanished ahead over the curve of the world. Now his command bucketed along alone in the tumbled grey waste.

The breeze got up and backed a trifle.

Every time he got all broody like this his thoughts reverted to what that French girl they'd picked up in a boat in the Atlantic had told him. She'd said her life had been saved by a German U-boat that took her off a sinking hulk. She'd been cared for. And the name of the commander of the U-boat, she had said, had been Baldur Wolz. At least, that was how Mitchell remembered it, and his old friendship with Baldur Wolz had made him wonder – could it be the same man?

Old Baldy – a U-boat commander?

That was his style. His father had been sunk at the tail end of the last war by a minesweeper of his own side. Baldur had spoken of that with some bitterness, not surprisingly.

Just suppose . . . Then Dick Mitchell closed his eyes against the wind, and opened them, just in case. Old Baldy – well, if they met through the fortunes of war, the duty each owed the other and each owed his country was plain.

As for Mitchell's own family, well, they tended to regard him as something of a black sheep. Typical of that was the way they complained about his MG churning up the gravel on the drive when he tore up to the front door on leave. The tennis courts saw a deal of him then, and the local pub; but he was, they said, a funny cuss, always itching to get back to his boats and to sea.

He sat on his seat on his bridge of his command, and for all the 'his' about it he might as well have been playing tennis back home. By the time he saw *Pathan* and *Kestrel* again, he surmised gloomily, all the fun and games would be over.

CHAPTER NINE

The crewmen tumbled up out of the fore hatch and ran along U-112's casing. The sea was just rough enough to make the process of securing fuel lines hazardous. Leaning over the bridge dodger, Wolz marked the men down there and watched them with an alert professional eye. He supposed, if he was honest with himself, that he would care if a man slipped on the casing and fell over the side, to be squashed between U-boat and tanker. But the thought did occur to him that he would be more annoyed at the slur on the seamanlike competence of the U-boat arm such a mishap would inevitably bring.

These were the thoughts of a young man embroiled in war, and they were not too pleasant. Wolz had been excused watchkeeping duty as he was about to leave *Kiruna*, and so he leaned over to get the best view of the boat that would be his new home.

He took out his case and selected a thin cheroot. He stuck the cigar into the corner of his mouth where it jutted up arrogantly, to the life itself. He was aware that he could easily be taken as a caricature of a Sea Wolf; but that did not bother him.

He went by results.

So far, and when all the accounts were in, he held the total of almost ninety thousand tons. That was not superbly good; but it was a good honest total. There would be more.

'Handsomely there, you – ' bellowed the boat's cox'n, a bear of a man with a black beard that was due for a trim, at the least. He shook a fist like a cooked ham. His men frapped out the pipeline smartly enough; but there was something about the way they moved, the air of them, that breezed a little disquiet up Wolz's spine.

They moved smartly, yes. But there was no snap about them.

Perhaps, he thought, they had been depth charged silly.

The little rubber airboat was bringing the U-boat commander across. His white cap gleamed in the weak Atlantic sunshine. Clouds flitted high, and shadows drew down around the ship and the U-boat, and then streaked away, grey and green across the water. They were in for a blow.

A shrill yell brought Wolz's instant attention away from the commander to his U-boat.

A man had fallen overboard.

'Grab him, you oaf!'

'Muttonhead! Hold on!'

Water sloshed up between the two steel hulls. The pipes had been laid out ready for transfer when the airboat was free. Then once the umbilical connection had been made the U-boat would drop back to nuzzle up astern.

The rubber boat reached the ladder at the ship's side.

It vanished from Wolz's view.

He looked down and saw the man struggling in the water.

That narrow gap looked dangerously narrow, sloshing in and out as the vessels moved in the sea.

A line was flung. The man made a frantic grab for it, and missed.

Wolz thought he could hear him yelling. But there was a racket going on in the boat and men were shouting and bawling, and the sea was splashing, and the uproar made him want to swear, if that was something he permitted himself.

The U-boat surged in the swell.

Wolz saw.

The steel saddle tanks ground in towards *Kiruna*'s side. The water thinned and narrowed like the light shutting off behind a closing door. He saw the man's white up turned face, the eyes and mouth black holes. He saw the two hulls slide in swoopingly, and touch with a loud crunching clang.

The sea roiled away and the U-boat sagged back.

Only a red stain showed on the water.

Wolz gripped on to his cigar.

Someone – someone was a stupid criminal idiot.

The last chopped off scream had been loud enough. He'd heard that shocked shriek clearly enough.

He clamped the cigar between his teeth. Anyway, if he'd been skippering that boat he'd have ferried the line across for the hosepipe first, and then come across himself afterwards.

He waited where he was. The accident was not his business, at least, not yet. If they wanted him to give evidence at the Court of Inquiry he would do so. He'd speak his mind.

He waited where he was. Miehle and the U-boat skipper would send for him when he was needed and when they had completed their business. He was, after all, merely a passenger.

'A bad business,' said Bekker, who was more or less up and about again.

'Yes.'

'Wouldn't do for us. Going on like that.'

'No.'

'Poor devil. He was crushed like a rotten apple.'

'Yes.'

Bekker turned away, his face pale.

'You won't be sorry to see me go?' said Wolz.

'What? Yes, of course. That is – '

'We each of us have to fight our own war.'

'True. I'd have that cox'n courtmartialled. He was criminally negligent.'

'The U-boat commander – '

'We all look after our own, I know.'

Now Wolz turned away. He wanted a few words with the Lutwaffe aircrew before he went. Nothing had been said about taking them off in U-112. He felt with a wry humour that they were glad of that.

And he could not suffer this conversation with Bekker a moment longer.

He felt the bitter resentment of his own thoughts of a moment ago. He'd been patronisingly assuming he'd feel more concern over a death of a seaman than the slur on the U-boat arm of the Kriegsmarine. Now the accident had happened. And he was involved in just that kind of inter-branch slanging match.

Not for the first time he realised just how war brutalised.

He went down the ladder to look out Trojer and Lindemann and bid them goodbye.

He stepped on to the deck and Trojer walked up, half-smiling, his Luftwaffe uniform looking more of a wreck than ever.

'So you're off, Wolz.'

'You're not coming with me?'

The Hauptmann screwed up his eyes.

'Over the top of the sea, not under it. That's my motto.'

'Lindemann – ?'

'He'll be along. If I didn't know any better I'd say you might have brought us bad luck. To be shot down like that.'

'You're alive – think of the girls and the champagne. I'll come out to see you at Bordeaux-Merignac.'

'Do that. We'll lay on a party.'

'Two parties, at least.'

Trojer noticed Wolz's cigar, frowned and started to say something. Then he noticed the cheroot was unlit, and the lines smoothed out between his eyes.

'Yes, one for you and one for us.'

'Sure you wouldn't like a quick trip home in a U-boat?'

'Quite sure. Orders –'

'Yes.'

'You're all packed and ready?'

'All there is to pack. *Kiruna* kitted me out a little.'

The fuel lines had been connected up now and the thick oily cylinders pulsed as the fuel was transferred. U-112 still wallowed along astern, and Wolz guessed her helmsman would be cursing away under his breath, and her engineer officer playing beautiful music with his diesels keeping the boat positioned. Fuelling at sea was a tricky job.

And a man's life had been lost, lost quite unnecessarily. That took a deal of the sunshine out of the day.

Then a shadow skittered across the sea and enveloped *Kiruna* and U-112 in an abrupt rainsquall. Vision was for a moment blotted out. The rain hit the deck with a loud spattering hiss. Wolz stepped back into the deck cabin. The darkness lowered down, grey and ominous.

After a few moments the squall passed. Light seeped back; but the clouds persisted, low and heavy, and the threat of more rain hung in the air with a damp and sodden feeling.

In a few short moments visibility had been drastically reduced.

The sun was a mere white patch, occasionally obscured, with a wider area of brightness about it. Wolz looked out across the sea. The breeze was getting up. Weather was coming in from the West, as usual, and it was likely to be a wild night.

Well, he should be snug in a U-boat by then.

He heard Miehle's voice before the Kapitän stepped out on to the deck.

'A regrettable occurrence. But life in the navy is hard. It is not for children.'

The hoarse penetrating voice answering made Wolz halt, stock still. His nostrils pinched in whitely. The bitten through cigar tumbled from his lips and bounced on the deck.

The man who stepped out after Miehle was short, short and spare. His eyes were two burning pits of brilliant blue. He looked arrogant, cock-sure, confident, his head tilted back not so much to see Miehle as in unaffected assumption of his own prowess. His white U-boat skipper's hat blazed with a brilliance so white it gleamed. His buttons shone. His decorations gleamed. He looked a young window-dummy rigged in oversize naval uniform.

Wolz stared at him.

The bulges leaped and jumped alongside Wolz's jaws.

Kapitänleutnant Adolf Forstner's jaws were covered by that thin strip of beard that was all he seemed able to grow when, like all U-boat men, he ceased to shave on patrol. His adolescent face bore new marks that betrayed the strain he had been under. He looked – he looked – Wolz forced himself to remain calm. This was the man who had chivvied and abused him, who had set bully-boys on him to beat him to a pulp. He looked what he was, a blot, an oaf, an apology for a human being and an excrescence as a U-boat commander.

Wolz just stood.

He could feel the movement of the ship. He could feel the breeze on his face. His hands hurt. He realised his fists were gripped so tightly they pained. He tried to make himself relax. But he could not. If he was to travel back to base in a U-boat commanded by Forstner his life would be a hell. He would in all probability not live to reach base.

Forstner was an active member of the Nazi Party. Wolz was slowly coming to realise that politics was not all there was to the Nazis, the white hope of Germany. And – he had believed in them whole-heartedly, as so many people had who were sick and tired of the way Germany had been pushed around. He still could point to many great achievements of the Nazi Party. But somehow, and with his experiences of that mysterious drive with Trudi, and that even more bizarre occurrence when her friends had been machine-gunned down in a quiet German country wood, he sensed machinations within that brilliant outer shell of the Party.

He had never been a party member. Siegfried, who had leaped at the chance of making something again of his

106

native land, had given up urging him to join, with an off hand remark that as he spent all his time at sea or in England the party wouldn't see much of him anyway.

Now, Wolz stared dumbly at Adolf Forstner, remembering the abject period in which he had served as the blot's Number One. Forstner would have him killed in U-112. That was not wild fantasy. That was a cold and horrible truth that Wolz had to face.

He made up his mind, instantly.

He would not sail back to base in U-112.

Not with Adolf Forstner in command.

Now Forstner turned towards him, moving with that turkey-cock strut. His lean face made the motions of a smile. He advanced and held out his hand.

'Baldur! How nice to see you! You are very welcome aboard U-112.'

The blot!

Wolz moistened his lips, and the butt of the cigar tumbled out. Miehle stared at him, frowning. Forstner went on smiling. His hand still stuck out. Forcing himself, taking the hand as though it were stinking offal, Wolz shook. The feel of Forstner's hand in his sickened him.

'You are all right, Herr Oberleutnant?' Miehle spoke sharply, that frown crinkling down between his eyebrows.

'Yes, thank you, Herr Kapitän.'

'Oh,' said Forstner, and he laughed a trifle too shrilly. 'Wolz is surprised to see me.'

'Yes –'

'We are old shipmates. Wolz was my First Lieutenant in U-45. We had a fine old time of it in Norway.' Forstner's smile remained, brilliant and painted. The blueness of his eyes blazed. 'There was a mix-up about taking command of U-55 – was it? Yes. A pity about that.'

Wolz had retrieved his composure now. He was not going aboard U-112 with this man. That would be going to his death.

This was not melodrama. It was a fact of which he

was completely and soberly assured.

He had to bring himself out of this desperate situation, and he had to make sure Miehle suspected nothing. There would be no deceiving Forstner. Wolz managed to widen his thin lips by a millimetre.

'You have had good hunting I trust?'

Some of that painted good-nature flaked off Forstner's narrow face.

'Oh, yes,' he said, and he spoke, Wolz saw, for the benefit of Miehle. 'Assuredly. But our eels misbehave and we have one left, and Kapitän Miehle has no replenishment for us.'

Wolz could not stop himself from speaking. 'But we use contact pistols now. They explode if you hit the target.'

Forstner's teeth showed as his lips stretched. His teeth looked very white contrasted with that strip of beard.

Miehle started forward, saying: 'Well, I'll leave you two to talk.' Then he halted. He looked back. 'The man who was lost overside. Can you let me know his name for my report?'

Forstner's lips clamped over his teeth. He kept his smile.

'Certainly, Herr Miehle. The moment I have made my enquiries into this unfortunate accident I shall inform you.'

Kiruna's captain nodded and walked off.

Slowly, Forstner took out his cigarette case, extracted a cigarette, put it between his lips, closed the case and replaced it in his pocket.

His steady blue gaze did not leave Wolz's face.

'I shall enjoy having you in U-112 with me, Wolz.'

The cigarette bobbled up and down as he spoke. He was, quite clearly, waiting for Wolz to proffer a light. Wolz stood, more easily now, his hands at his sides. He made no move to take out his lighter.

At last Forstner lit his own cigarette. He blew the smoke out, a thin blue-grey plume. His lips bunched up to blow and they glistened red.

'Oh, yes, I shall look forward to it very much.'

Just how that cigarette was not pulped back on to those squashed red lips by a knuckly fist, Wolz did not know.

He restrained himself.

He nodded.

'You will be refuelled and away today?'

'Oh, if these oafs do their job properly.'

'I see.'

'Perhaps you might go down and assist them? I remember the men seemed to jump more when you appeared.'

Wolz eyed him. He could refuse – barely. But he was prepared to go along with the formalities for as long as was decent. He would fabricate an excuse at the last minute so as to prevent himself from going aboard U-112. He'd fall down the damned companionway if necessary. There would be no facilities in the U-boat for a man with a busted leg.

'Well? I am waiting?'

'Very good.'

'I want to get clear,' Forstner went on, blowing smoke. And he said something that made Wolz open his eyes wide. 'I want to be well away before *Bismarck* gets here. I have orders and I know those bastard English.'

'*Bismarck*?'

Before Forstner could react to the tone in Wolz's voice, he said quickly; 'I understand. It is a pity there are no suitable torpedoes aboard. *Bismarck* will need all the help we can give her. If she can get among a convoy . . .'

'Quite. Well, Wolz, go on down and get busy!'

As he left the blot standing there filled with smug anticipation; even over his own worries, Wolz saw what *Kiruna* was about, what was taking place. Raeder and Hitler had at last sanctioned a raid by the biggest ship of all! *Bismarck* was unsinkable, so the experts said. And she was out! She must be. And *Kiruna* was just one of a chain of supply ships.

Then Wolz frowned.

Kiruna was way down south. Well, that must mean that the big ship wouldn't try for the return to Germany but would join *Scharnhorst* and *Gneisenau* in Brest. What a formidable battle squadron that would be! Wolz couldn't know all the plans, of course; but he could see enough to know that a moment of decisive importance approached in the war at sea.

Then the reality of his own situation overwhelmed him. All that fake friendship, that cheerful comradeship, from Adolf Forstner had been a mask. It was a carefully contrived cover to impress Miehle so that when Baldur Wolz was reported as being dead in U-112, Forstner could exhibit all the sorrow of a friend. The inquiry would reveal whatever the macabre facts were in the death of Baldur Wolz, and it would also show that Forstner was a friend of the deceased.

Forstner, already, was covering his tracks.

No. Wolz was absolutely convinced from his own personal experience that Forstner would have him put out of the way. If he took passage in U-112 for base, he would never reach home alive.

CHAPTER TEN

HMS *Pathan* swirled up through the sea like a lean hungry hound dog and the Aldiss chattered frantically from her bridge.

Mitchell looked at his yeoman of signals.

He hadn't expected to see the Tribal destroyer again for some time. But *Pathan's* course had brought her up from the north, and *Kestrel* showed, keeping company, away to the west.

Mitchell smiled.

He smiled a little nastily.

So the two blustering Fleet destroyers had not found their quarry. That was most interesting.

The signal coming in from *Pathan* was a long one.

Perhaps, surmised Mitchell, Elliot had decided to let him know what was going on. It looked like it. The two big destroyers had failed to find what they were looking for, and if *Bruiser* was to assist then her commander would have to know what to look out for in this waste of waters.

When, at last, Dick Mitchell read the signal handed to him by the yeoman, he understood. He whistled.

Andy Stevens looked curious.

'Damned Jerry supply ship somewhere around here, Number One. They've located her radio signals on the direction finding equipment; but that's accurate to far too wide a latitude. It's my guess those odd-looking aerials in *Pathan* are some new-fangled radio-direction finding gear.'

'Very likely, sir.'

'We're ordered to form a search pattern to the south

and west. I'd also guess that that is the place *Pathan* least expects to bump the Jerry.'

'He could be wrong, sir. We picked him up steaming in from the north. He'd found nothing there.'

'Quite so, Number One.'

Mitchell called down to Sub-Lieutenant Garvin Fellowes.

'Pilot. Work a search pattern to the south west. Take in all you can but keep it more to the south than west.'

At Stevens' raised eyebrow Mitchell went on calmly: 'There's a Jerry supply ship out there somewhere and our two friends have failed to find her to the north of the line.'

'Understood, sir,' came up the Pilot's young voice.

'You think – ?' began Stevens.

'Always a dangerous game, Number One. Thinking.'

'Yes, sir.'

'But we were steering two three five. North and south of that line – and I'm betting it's south. Captain Elliot evidently thought it was north.'

'He has gear fitted to check it out, sir.'

'Maybe. He also has a tin ear from Dunkirk.'

Mitchell gave the size of the area he wanted to search first and the Pilot very quickly laid off a course. Mitchell was impressed with Sub Fellowes. He knew his stuff. *Bruiser* leaned gently over in the water as she swung around to port and Mitchell took her into the first leg of the search pattern.

The weather, which had been threatening all manner of diabolical liberties with a small ship now blew hard and then blew soft. Typical Spring weather in the Atlantic. The blow, when it came, would be a corker.

Mist patches blew past the bridge. Mitchell looked ahead. The horizon extended there as it extended to port and starboard and astern. Always, the prow of his ship pointed to the horizon and he drove on and, one day, he'd fall off the edge. The conceit was not all that foolish; falling off the edge could come with a Jerry torpedo in his engine room.

The sea's grey-green immensity held him in its eternal embrace. That was sometimes a a clammy embrace. The clouds lowered down and reduced visibility where they touched the sea's surface. Then the embrace became all too real.

His steward brought up a cup of kai which he drank far too hot. He clasped the mug in his hands, feeling the warmth, and as ever marvelled that the heat in the cocoa remained after it had been brought to the bridge.

The lookouts had been told to look out. That was their job. No need to impress on them that now they were looking for a ship. That might all too easily take their attention off the little black stick, the flicker of white, that was a U-boat's periscope.

The weather was patchy now. Difficult.

'Yeoman,' said Mitchell, rousing himself. 'You'd better double up the lookouts. Keep 'em on their toes. In this muck they might miss seeing *Hood*.'

'Aye, aye, sir.'

He'd meant the remark as a kind of joke that would take the sting out of double look-out duty. *Hood* was big enough to be seen anytime. But he had no intention of allowing *Pathan* and *Kestrel* any chance at all of bawling him out. If the Nazi supply ship was in his sector, he intended to find her.

He looked around his bridge. Everything proceeded. By this time he'd got *Bruiser* ticking over as he would like and the sight of his bridge, and the men at their posts, the sight and sound of ordered activity, gave him a comfortingly warm glow within himself.

To be on the bridge of a destroyer in wartime – wasn't that the acme of his ambition?

And, after *Bruiser* – what? If there was an after.

That little Wren with the wheat-coloured hair in Plymouth. If she got her transfer to Liverpool, as she had threatened him, laughing . . . Monica. Nice. Do no good to be serious with any girl, though. As he had always done, play the field. If you looked at his future dispassionately, you would have to say he would be highly likely to spend the rest of his war in escorts. That would be the way of it. Better that, he supposed than the anonymity of a battleship. Here he was king.

A lookout sang out, and another echoed him. A sighting obtained on the starboard bow – Mitchell had expected the Jerry to appear on the port side on this leg. Then –

'It's *Kestrel*, sir!'

Moments later *Pathan* appeared from the murk and shot on across *Bruiser*'s bows.

No intemperate Aldiss demands signalled. The two Fleet destroyers bore on, spuming spray, smashing their way through the sea, heading south fast.

'If they want me to search here, what the hell do they mean by barging in?' said Mitchell wrathfully.

'They looked in a hurry, sir . . .'

'They did Number One. And if our theory about those fancy aerials is right – Pilot! I am changing course due south.' He rapped out the steering instructions, and went on: 'Plot that into your search in case we draw a blank.'

'Aye, aye, sir. It's not too much off track, in any case.'

'Good.'

Fifteen minutes later the first gunshots boomed from the mist ahead.

Kiruna towed U-112 as the refuelling proceeded. The thick fuel lines pulsed. The mist dropped down and then cleared and a watery sun winked myopically across the damp decks.

Wolz put his thoughts to the matter in hand – not that it was of great consequence. But one man had already tragically died and that was something Wolz hated. Stupid waste of human life depressed him.

At sea human life could so easily be snuffed out.

That was what Forstner would say – afterwards.

Miehle for all his stiff-necked big-ship manner was a decent enough man and Wolz considered appealing to him.

What could he say? Please, Herr Kapitän, I do not wish to go aboard U-112 because the commander will have me killed.

Miehle would consider he was raving.

No, better to have a minor mishap so that he would have to stay in the sick bay aboard *Kiruna*. That was a miserable prospect. But it was better than being stuffed into a torpedo tube and fired out at fourteen metres.

If Forstner managed to have him killed in such a way that no suspicious marks showed, the oaf might well keep him in the torpedo tube for burial ashore. It was a common practice. Wolz didn't like it. Far better to bury a man at sea and say whatever was necessary over him than keep him stuffed into a torpedo tube. The mess for the dockside men to clear out was fierce — fierce and foul and stinking.

Often the water swelled the corpse up so much it wouldn't come out properly, and had to be chipped out.

Wolz shook himself.

Forstner, the blot, could not be allowed —

A smashing crash and a shower of cold water slashing all across Wolz sent him to his knees on the deck. His head rang.

Another almighty crash bellowed up. Dazedly, he saw a waterspout erupt from the sea a cable's length away. He saw a lifeboat splintered from its davits as though a mighty invisible wind had breathed fire across it. That concussion when it came knocked him the other way.

Kiruna was under fire!

Men were running and yelling. The wooden deck house collapsed as men ripped the supports away. The gun revealed was a 10.5 cm and it gleamed with purposeful power. The crew tore at it, freeing it for action. Other men raced across the deck with ammunition from the ready use lockers.

Wolz saw that they knew what they were doing and he could leave them to get on with it. He was just a passenger.

Another almighty crash belched bits and pieces into

the air. He ducked. The upperworks of *Kiruna* billowed smoke. Tangled wreckage dangled. He saw a man's body hurled upwards in the air, gyrating, and as it span so it shed strings and streamers of blood.

He tore his gaze away and looked over the side.

Over there and half-hidden by spray and the speed of her passage a long, low, grey shape, hungry and powerful, sliced through the sea.

As that shape rose to a wave so Wolz saw the red flicker of flame from two forrard guns.

He recognised the ship at a single glance.

An English destroyer! A Tribal!

The same sort of hunting dog as that infamous *Cossack*.

The shells slammed into *Kiruna*. They struck into the hull. And, in that instant, two more sledge-hammer blows belted the ship as the two after guns scored. But Tribals had twin 4.7″ guns in their shields. The second salvo came in with devastating speed, shredding the German ship. Bits of steel plating flew through the air.

A man carrying a 10.5 cm shell had no time to scream. The razor-edged chunk of steel sliced him in two.

His body toppled to the right and the shell bounced and rolled on the deck. His legs fell to the left, twitching.

Only a red greasiness welled between.

Kiruna was done for.

Another English destroyer appeared momentarily in the shifting veils of mist. Wolz caught a bemused glimpse of her. He thought she had only one funnel. Then six twinkling spots of red flickered luridly from her – four forrard and two aft.

Kiruna staggered. Smoke beat down in the mist, choking, as the shells slammed in . . .

The ship was on fire.

A group of yelling men had swung a lifeboat out and it went down in the falls with a swoop. Wolz didn't see it hit the water; but it seemed to be all right as the men started sliding down. He saw an officer with them, and judged the crew were not panicking. As another shell slammed into the hull beneath his feet, and chunks of debris flew up with a geysering spout of water, he felt that panic might be considered the order of the day. The crew had to abandon ship, that was certain.

The sea had lessened. The swathing banks of mist had brought a slight cessation in the heave of the sea, the breeze had dropped away. Under the coils of mist the sea looked oily.

Smoke billowed down. An inversion in the air was bringing the black clouds down in smothering folds. But the ship burned and the ominous crackle and hiss of flames broke up abaft the funnel. The mast went by the board bringing down the aerials in a lacering network of wires across the upperworks and deck. Men were racing to free the other lifeboats.

The 10.5 cm had fired without visible effect.

Wolz began to think he'd better go across and see if he had a better eye to lay the gun.

He started to move and was slammed back . . . He felt the buffet in his chest as though he'd been run into by a steam loco gone haywire. He sprawled across the deck.

The 10.5 cm lifted into the air bodily off its mounting. It turned over. It flew away. Wolz saw it all as though in slow motion. The smash of flame hit him as he lay there, and the acrid stink enveloped him. He gagged. His eyes were running water. His head shook. The gun had been struck squarely by an English shell. The noise pounded at him as though he was in a steel coffin hammered by iron bars.

The two Luftwaffe men appeared, staggering along the deck in the smoke. They were yelling.

Lindemann, the navigator, still hobbled a bit on his wounded leg; but it had mended enough so that in this emergency he could run for the boats.

Trojer, the pilot, was hauling Lindemann along.

They saw Wolz just sitting up on the deck, holding

his head. In Wolz's skull all the bells of Cologne Cathedral were ringing together, only not quite together, so that the reverberations set up a dissonance that gonged from one side of his head to the other.

'You – all right – Wolz?'

'Come on, then.'

Wolz could feel the ship beneath him. He knew the English were shooting 4.7" shells at *Kiruna*. They were about a 12 cm shell in German measurement. He did not think the ship would go down just yet, and the feel of her told him she was not settling any further in the water. But in his condition he could be wrong. He was confused. The smoke and the noise rattled and shattered inside his head. His face felt as though it had been scraped raw.

There was no hope for the gun's crew. Their bits and bloody pieces were scattered over the deck and washing in the sea.

'Come on, Wolz!'

'Yes . . .'

It was extraordinarily difficult to get up.

He felt as though he'd been drinking his uncle's best French champagne all night – from Lottie's shoe, in all probability. He had a monumental hangover. He put his hands flat on the deck, and he laughed, and tried to get up, and fell over.

The English had stopped shooting.

Vaguely, he wondered why that was.

The Walther P.38 automatic holstered at his waist was digging into his side. He lay on the deck. He couldn't get up.

But he had to get up.

Had to.

The ship was going to sink any minute – wasn't it?

'Wolz! *Wolz!*'

'All – right.' He heard his voice, like the scrape of a spade against a coffin. 'Find – a boat.'

So this was what it was like in a sinking ship.

He'd sent enough to the bottom, as a U-boat commander.

Now it was his turn.

He tried to stand up. No, no it wasn't his turn. There was too much to do. There was Lottie – and Heidi, there was Mariza, there was Trudi. As ever he couldn't think straight of Cousin Lisl. There were his cousins. No, there was a war to fight. He couldn't go down with a ship, not now.

Particularly not, especially not – a surface ship!

If he was to be sunk, he'd be sunk in a U-boat, like any decent U-boat skipper.

The alarm clock ringing insanely in his head began to dim and blur. He could see more clearly. He stood up.

The ship was a shambles.

She was burning. If she didn't sink shortly from the hits along her waterline she'd burn out and then sink.

The sound of champagne corks popping made him frown.

Odd . . .

He looked owlishly towards the deckhouse.

Men were running there, men in blue uniforms, like sailors. Men with canvas gaiters and funny round helmets – he gaped.

Then, shaking, he hauled out the Walther automatic and started to totter towards the deckhouse.

Dick Mitchell saw the livid gun flashes streaking through the mist.

He saw four flashes sparkle out and then another four.

'That's *Pathan* at full bore!' he shouted.

A moment later three double flashes scored the darkling air.

'And that's *Kestrel*!'

The answering shots seemed to sprout from the sea almost alongside.

The mist drifted thickly there and the sea lifted in

oily patterns. Mitchell strained his eyes. *Bruiser* had run on along the track and the gunfire had lured her like the scent of the chase. Another long tongue of flame slashed the mist ahead.

'That's the Jerry, sir!' shouted Stevens. 'It's got to be!'

'Yes. And we're nearly on top of her.'

Mitchell rang down the engines, and even then he had a quick mental image of the Chief grunting that he could take some of the pressure off. *Bruiser* began to lose way. Mitchell felt forward carefully.

Even then, he almost piled his ship up on the German. The thickening blot of blackness ahead coalesced.

'Hard a'port!'

Bruiser swung around.

They could see the fires now, beginning to flare up. Immense crashings and bangings echoed across the oily water. The German ship abruptly materialised.

'My God!' yelled Stevens. 'We're right on top of her!'

'Stop engines!'

'Stop engines!'

Bruiser ran on.

Mitchell looked carefully and the instructions issued to all captains popped clearly into his mind.

'Number One! Muster a boarding party. Full rig. Stand no nonsense! You know what we want – if the Jerries haven't burned all the books already. Jump!'

'Aye, aye, sir!'

The destroyer wallowed as her way came off. Mitchell gave sharp precise instructions to the quartermaster and the ship eased herself alongside. The supply ship towered over them, and the smoke gusted down, making them cough.

Lines were flung.

Sailors jumped on to the deck. Their steel helmets always, Mitchell considered, made sailors look odd, as though they were playing at soldiers. But the Lee Enfields in their fists meant business.

They were able to scramble aboard on to the German's well-deck forward. No one, thank God, fell into the sea.

Bruiser hung against the German's forward port bow. She'd only just avoided what would have been a head-on collision. Lines were thrown. The boarding party vanished on to the deck.

Mitchell stared up, and his lips ricked back.

'Fetch my revolver,' he said to his steward.

He felt that to be a theatrical gesture. But the Admiralty instructions had been quite explicit. Anything that would give a clue to the German cyphers, *anything*, would be invaluable. Number One was sound. He could be trusted . . . A captain did not leave his ship to head a boarding party . . .

Mitchell fretted. What the hell was going on in that ship?

The Fleet destroyers had ceased fire, so they must have seen him go alongside through the patchy mist.

Mitchell put his hands in his pockets and thrust down. He stuck his chin out. There was the sound of shooting. Smoke gushed down as the ship burned. He'd have to shove off soon . . . Where the hell was Stevens?

At last, and because he was Ram Mitchell, a bit of a maniac, and, also, because he understood the importance of cracking the Jerry codes, he couldn't stand it any more.

'You have the ship, Lieutenant Colledge. I won't be long.'

'But, sir!' protested Colledge, the second, an RNVR officer who knew more about law than the sea. 'You can't –'

'I can and I damned well will. If the fires get too close, push off. Hang around for us for as long as you can. But do not hazard the ship. *Pathan* will give you orders.'

'Aye, aye, sir – but – '

But Mitchell was gone.

The whole midships of *Kiruna* was enveloped in smoke.

The flames bit up; but the combustibles gave off more smoke than flame. The stern was cut off from the bows by the smoke. And by the way the ship surged sluggishly in the sea, she had shipped enough water to ensure she'd sink before the fires broke out of control.

Andy Stevens wanted to get this madness over as quickly as possible.

'Get aft into deckhouse, chief, and be slippy about it.'

'Aye, aye, sir.'

GPO Millbanks, a rolling hunk of muscle, bellowed his men on and they ran up the ladder and into the smoke, Stevens at their head. The radio shack was a mass of flame and smoke. Just below it, then . . .

Dark figures ran from the cabin ahead. The smoke swatched the two sides. As Stevens lifted his service revolver and shot heavily at those running figures he found time to be thankful for that. If the Jerries had machine pistols it would be a dicey business . . .

The rifles rattled at his side. The men surged on with a yell. Smoke made them all cough and choke. But they broke through into the cabin. One wall burned. Papers and books and a mish-mash of wreckage lay scattered wildly.

'Grab it all. Don't miss anything, even if it's a laundry list.' Number One ordered the men into the deckhouse and yelled at the CPO 'Chief! Let's try the next one!'

They ran aft followed by those ratings not detailed to collect everything from that cabin. The next cabin was a mass of smoke. Stevens barged in and a moment later emerged, scarlet of face, his cheeks distended, whooping.

'No go there,' he spluttered out when he could talk.

They ran on and reached the end of the deckhouse. Half a dozen dismembered bodies strewed the deck, splashed with blood. Empty shell cases rolled with the drunken surge of the vessel.

'Into that cabin, chief!'

'Aye, aye, sir.'

They were free of much of the smoke now. Stevens whipped into the last cabin. His revolver snouted ahead; but the men at whom he had fired previously had not reappeared. If they were hanging around in the smoke . . .

'Musta been in that first cabin, sir,' said Chief Millbanks.

'Right. Back the way we came.'

The davits were turned and empty. Lines dangled to the sea. Stevens did not go any further aft. He felt confident that the radio shack was in flames and unapproachable. He had found a mass of documents in the cabin immediately beneath. There was no point in hanging around; the ship was due to founder at any moment.

Led by Stevens the boarding party plunged once more into the smoke.

The men detailed to collect everything appeared. Stevens went into the cabin and personally checked that no papers had been overlooked. He stared about, the revolver in his fist, his steel helmet cocked to one side, his eyes raking the cabin.

The burning wall had been almost eaten through. Paint bubbled and the smoke choked out, flat and greasy. Pretty soon the whole cabin would be a single mass of flame. If they had found anything of value, then they had been very lucky.

The steel bulkhead beyond the wooden walling glowed.

Three metal cylinders fell from a wall bracket. Stevens glanced at them. He had no idea what they were. But the skipper had said anything, and Stevens had enough nous to know that strange-looking objects like this would not be placed in this cabin without good reason.

'Grab those, chief. Then back to *Bruiser*.'

'You heard the officer! On the double!'

With a last look around, Stevens left the cabin.

He saw dim figures through smoke aft and took a couple of quick shots at them. The smoke thickened. No answering shots snapped back at him. The chief was bawling the ratings forward.

Then the funnel fell.

The noise smashed into a bedlam of sound.

Stevens thought the world had fallen in on top of him. He ran on towards the ladder leading down to the forward well deck. Black smoke, thick and sooty, engulfed everything. The men were coughing and spitting, wiping their eyes.

'Over to the starboard ladder! We'll get across the fo'c's'le!'

'Aye, aye, sir!'

They burst across to the starboard side where the smoke thinned just a little, enough for them to see the ladder down was intact if bent. One after the other they shinnied down. Stevens went last.

He looked back.

The ship was in one hell of a mess.

The funnel draped across the deck and smoke and soot and muck poured out. Fires were now spreading up in real earnest. A tiny breeze cats-pawed across his face. It blew the smoke away from the port side and into his eyes, and he cursed, before dropping down the ladder.

Chief Millbanks was there, looking belligerent, his rifle snouting.

A dead German lay sprawled, blood seeping from a hole in his chest.

Millbanks held a nasty-looking machine pistol.

'Trophy, chief?'

'Something like that, sir. He'd have had us all – he got Timmins, poor sod – beggin' your pardon, sir.'

'Well done, chief.' Stevens could imagine what had been going on down here whilst he had been gawking up aloft. 'Let's clear off. The skipper will be having kittens.'

They ran across the well deck, cutting back to the port side. There was, thankfully, no need to go on to the fo'c's'le. *Bruiser* was there, still waiting for them, and the lines looked very thin and frail – but the old ship was there.

'Aboard with you, and step lively!'

Andy Stevens, First Luff of HMS *Bruiser*, shepherded his boarding party back aboard. He hoped he had done well. They had enough papers – but, as he had said, they could all be Jerry laundry lists.

Trojer yelled but his words were lost in the bedlam. Smoke gushed down and partially obscured those hurrying figures with the canvas gaiters and blue uniforms and silly helmets. Wolz recognised the shape of the helmets.

Lindemann almost fell over as Trojer let go.

Wolz tried to aim his automatic and the smoke blurred his vision.

Someone shot at him from the smoke, the bullets going whack, whack, whack past him. He could see nothing to shoot at.

'English!' shouted Trojer, his voice thin and attenuated.

'My leg!' shrieked Lindemann.

'We must –' Wolz said. He shook his head. 'We must stop them.'

The ship lurched.

He started forward along the port side.

'We must get to a boat!' Trojer yelled in his ear as he went past. Among all the bells ringing in there the Luftwaffe man's voice sounded like a ghost keening in a graveyard.

'You – go. Navy business.'

'Help me up!' shrieked Lindemann.

Wolz staggered on into the smoke.

Everything fell down.

The noise mounted to such a pitch of clanging and gonging and batterings he halted, dazed. The world turned black. Soot puffed everywhere. He guessed what had happened.

The funnel had at last gone by the board.

Through the murk the glare of fire above told him the radio shack blazed fiercely. The smoke wafted away a trifle and he saw flames spouting from the forrard cabins. He'd never get through there. The cabin containing the Enigma machine in its secret hidey-hole crackled and roared with fire.

If the English hadn't already taken what they'd come for they'd take it now. He couldn't get through and he judged the English had gone. They must have a boat forrard somewhere. They might as well be on the Moon, for all the good –

As fast as he could he backtracked and went around the starboard side. Maybe he could get through that way. If he could, his duty was to stop the English.

The smoke choked less thickly here. The ship moved under him sluggishly now, tired and beaten, ready to welcome the inrush of the sea.

The crackle of an M.P.38 burst out and was abruptly stilled in the heavier crack of a rifle.

Smoke obscured his forward vision.

And that damned breeze switched about again and blew smoke the other way, forcing him back. He stumbled away, his arm over his face. No chance, now, of getting forrard.

But, if the fitful breeze had blown the smoke away from the port side it was his duty to try one more last time. He had to. The movement seemed to have given him energy. His head no longer rang so fearsomely. His face was black and streaked with tears. But he still had the automatic and the ship was not gone yet.

Looking aft he could just make out Trojer assisting Lindemann to rise. The thought occurred to him that the two Luftwaffe men must be all at sea in this burning and sinking ship. The thought amused him. He felt his lips stretch. All at sea . . .

He rounded the aft corner of the deckhouse and saw a man in the act of turning around to go forrard again. The tendrils of smoke still blew; but Wolz saw the broad blue-clad shoulders, and the naval cap. For a betraying moment he couldn't tell if that man was German or

English. Sailors wear blue . . .

A movement just above him made him look up quickly.

The smoke, driven by the freakish breeze, blew away from the deckhouse. The ladder had been burned away, and smouldered, shiny and black. A man crouched there. Wolz saw him.

It was Adolf Forstner.

Wolz saw.

Forstner lifted his Luger. He aimed at the broad back of the naval officer starting forward.

Forstner fired.

He shot three times.

The man flung up his arms and toppled sideways. In his right hand he gripped a big old-fashioned looking revolver. He did not drop the gun. He fell. As he fell he twisted around and hit the deck on his left shoulder.

The revolver spat flame.

Forstner screamed.

He fell forward. His arms flew out and the Luger spun away. He crashed into the deck, face first, smearingly. His white-topped cap flopped off. He twitched and the English officer shot him again as he lay there.

Forstner's body jumped under the impact of the slug.

Wolz looked over Forstner at the Englishman and he lifted his automatic. He took a pace forward.

The two men, one standing with a Walther automatic, the other lying on the deck in his own blood desperately gripping a Webley revolver, stared at each other.

They looked.

'Dick!'

'Baldy!'

'You're dying –'

'What – happened to my – men?'

Macabre, unreal, insane . . . What they had to say to each other, and they talked of death and of duty . . .

'They went forrard on the starboard side –'

'Baldy! I don't feel anything. Am I dying?'

'I think so. How –'

'You in – U-boats, Baldy?'

'Yes.'

'I – thought so.'

Smoke blew and Wolz waved his left hand irritably. He did not want to lose sight of Dick Mitchell now.

'Met a – French girl – said she knew you.'

'I remember –'

'We had some times, eh, old lad?'

'Yes. Your ship?'

'Can't tell you that.' Mitchell's head lolled foolishly. He slumped down. He still held the revolver. The Walther still pointed at his heart.

'Remember the commandant's – wife's – knickers?'

'They flew very well –'

'Didn't they – just – I don't feel anything. All this blood . . .

Wolz licked his lips. What did you say in an insane situation like this?

Mitchell looked up; but Wolz guessed he could see very little.

'I shot – your pal. Sorry about that; but he shot me.'

'You did me a favour, Dick.'

Mitchell slumped down further and his legs stupidly shook as they extended straight out, like a drunk's. He tried to lift his head. His uniform cap lay at his side, almost floating in blood.

'Goodbye, Dick. I –'

'The ship's done for, Baldy. You'd – better hop it – PDQ.'

'Yes. PDQ as you say.'

'We had some good times –'

Mitchell's eyes closed. The Webley toppled from his fingers. He lay flat, unseeing, unmoving, and his blood glistened in the light of the flames of the sinking ship.

Wolz turned away, and then, foolishly, swung back.

Gravely, he put the automatic into his left hand. He lifted his hand in salute – a naval salute – and then he started aft.

He didn't even think of Forstner until he had his hand under Lindemann's armpit and with Trojer on the other side was urging them towards the stern of the ship.

Kiruna shuddered.

Forstner could go to the hell he deserved.

Baldur Wolz had seen a friend shot by Forstner and knew he would have been the next. He would think about that tomorrow. Right now he had a U-boat to reach, and a couple of Luftwaffe dandies to shepherd. The thought of the U-boat gave him strength.

CHAPTER ELEVEN

U-112 was not a happy boat.

That in no way surprised Baldur Wolz.

He had had experience of serving with the late Adolf Forstner as commander, and he knew the sourness the blot brought with him.

Oberleutnant Kurt Grunberger, the First Officer, had taken over command of U-112. By virtue of four months seniority he had the right over Wolz. Wolz accepted the situation philosophically. He was alive to the knowledge that but for the death of Forstner, this Grunberger would regard him, Wolz, in a very different light.

Nothing had, apparently, come to light about the absence of the commander of U-112. Forstner had not returned aboard the U-boat, and they had been forced to push off when *Kiruna* sank. The English had steamed off at high speed. The mist patches had effectively prevented any sight of the lifeboats, and Wolz wondered just how many men had got away from the supply ship. A search revealed nothing, which was strange. For all Grunberger knew, these three, Wolz and the two Luftwaffe men, were the sole survivors.

If Wolz knew the English at all he fancied they'd send a further search party out to pick up the boats. For one thing, they'd want information. No doubt, as so often happened in these situations, the English had steamed off in a real flap about the presence of U-boats.

U-112, with one eel left in her stern tube, was not going to cause them a deal of trouble. But, of course, they could not know that.

'B.d.U. was not at all happy, Wolz,' said Grunberger.

They sat in the wardroom of the U-boat. The familiar stinks of a boat at sea filled Wolz's nostrils. At first he, a hardened U-boat man, had noticed the effluvium with distaste. But he accustomed himself to it with rapidity. The two Luftwaffe men were still being sick.

'I'm not surprised. It was a shambles.'

'We must hope that Operation Rheinübung has not been compromised.'

Wolz had learned it all now.

'There are other supply ships. The English can't possibly have captured or sunk them all.'

'I trust you are right. Our orders are clear.'

The other officers and the crewmen in U-112 all seemed to Wolz to move and talk in a peculiar shuffling whispering way. They all looked uneasy. Well, under the sea unease was a mild word to describe the feelings of men trapped in iron coffins, awaiting the onslaught of depth charges. But there was something else in this boat. As he had sensed within a very short time of boarding her, U-112 was not a happy boat.

Wolz heard the story of U-112's cruise so far, and learned she had had lean pickings. The eels, apparently, did still misbehave, and he remembered those two unaccountable misses on his own last patrol.

Now B.d.U. ordered them east to join a patrol line forming four hundred and fifty miles or so west of St. Nazaire. The raiding cruise of *Bismarck*, on which so many hopes had been raised, had received a setback. The news of the sinking of HMS *Hood* was received with wild acclamation. They played the gramophone and when Grunberger put on patriotic music, Wolz did not object. He recalled *Hood*, the marvel and the beauty and the power of her. And now she was a twisted burnt hulk beneath the sea.

As the messages came in and they steamed eastwards as fast as the twin diesels could push them, the story unfolded. *Bismarck* would make for Brest. There were aircraft attacks. The fantastic amount of subdivisioning in the battleship prevented a single torpedo from sinking her. She steamed on for base, and the English shadowed her and called up their own powerful fleet units from ports a thousand miles away.

Wolz was fully conscious of the importance of the events now taking place in the Atlantic.

U-112 had one torpedo left. If that could be used to stop a British battleship or *Ark Royal*, they would have struck a blow that might save the day for *Bismarck*.

Their own radio picked up some of *Bismarck*'s signals. They followed the unfolding drama. Everyone was tense and jumpy. The atmosphere in the boat was electric.

'Once they get within range of the Luftwaffe,' said Trojer. 'We'll put so many aircraft in action the English won't stand a chance.'

'She has to reach that point yet,' said Grunberger. He was a plumpish man with a doughy face, and eyes of a dull green colour. He still hadn't quite realised he was in command of U-112. He gave his orders and the boat ran, and the watches changed. Observing the Oberleutnant, Wolz could see plainly enough he was still functioning with the baleful shadow of Forstner peering over his shoulder. Grunberger must have led a dog's life – and yet . . . Wolz frowned. Perhaps this dough-faced individual had been a crony of Forstner's, hand-picked, like him a dedicated Nazi. Perhaps Wolz shouldn't feel sorry at all for Grunberger . . .

It was difficult to tell with the peculiar situation in the boat, with *Bismarck* making her run for safety, with the two Luftwaffe men aboard, with Grunberger's own doughy personality to contend with.

There were a number of incidents which, petty in themselves, added up to a kind of doughy incompetence in the boat that Wolz – or any self-respecting U-boat skipper – would not tolerate.

Trojer, having overcome the worst of his sickness, seemed possessed of a curious nervous vitality at odds with his navigator. Lindemann's leg pained him; but he was in no danger. Yet he slumped down in a corner of the wardroom and refused to take any interest in anything. Wolz remembered his actions at the time the Focke Wulf had been shot down. Then the navigator had acted with determination, despite being wounded.

This was just another example of the way a U-boat could suck the vitality from an otherwise healthy and courageous man. Manning a U-boat called for a very special set of qualities. Not all men possessed them.

U-112 was a brand new U-boat, and this was her first cruise. She was a Type VIIB, similiar to the boats of the aces, and new though she was already Wolz could see unmistakable signs in her that worried him. He decided to take a politic tack at first with Grunberger. After all, U-boat officers received a gruelling and thorough training, and duds were chucked out, so that Grunberger must have gone through the mill and must know what commanding a U-boat was all about.

The U-boat numbers 112 to 115 had originally been allocated to the Type XI back in 1938. The boats would have been large and fast and have been fitted with powerful guns and a seaplane. None had been laid down. What was needed, it had been seen, was not a boat to fight the last war but a fighting craft to tackle the problems of the next.

Wolz thought of his old U-55 and the sad state of that famous boat, and contrasted his command with this spanking new boat that was already sway-backed from misuse. All the silly, tiny, infuriating little things that were continually going wrong in a boat went wrong in U-112 – only ten times more often than usual. Trifles, most of them might be. But a man's life, the safety of the whole boat, could go smash on a trifle.

The Leitender Ingenieur, Leutnant Hechler, struck Wolz as being a man so strangely unsure of himself, for all his theoretical knowledge, that it was a miracle the boat ran at all. Of course, that was exaggeration. Wolz suspected darkly that the repressive shadow of Forstner had been at work here. The chief engineer responsible for the diesels, Stabsobermaschinist Wohl, seemed a good man, and to anyone with eyes to see Wohl carried out more duties than his station or rank warranted.

The big bear of a cox'n, Meckel, was a Stabsoberbootsmann, and he made sure no one overlooked that important fact. The boat was well-supplied with relatively high-ranking officers and men, and again Wolz conjectured that Forstner's friends had served him well. He only hoped there would be no repercussions when they reached base.

Forstner had died at sea, in action, and that ought to be an end to it.

The port diesel gave trouble and Wohl sweated blood over it before he got it running smoothly again. That delay cost them five hours. U-112 punched into the sea, heading east for the patrol line, and the radio crackled out brief pungent messages. They learned of Bismarck's dash for safety, and the frantic efforts of the English to catch her.

The West group of U-boats had been called in. From what Wolz could make out most of them were low on fuel and out of eels. But their mere presence would deter the English. A U-boat had only to lurk, unseen and potentially deadly, below the surface, and the English reacted like skittish horses at too high fences.

The nor' westerly persisted and freshened and U-112 tended to wallow in an ungainly fashion with the seas pounding in on to her stern. Wolz stood his watch on the bridge, fitting into the watch-keeping duties, and the boat rolled and surged across the sea.

He had to quell an unpleasant tendency on the part of the lookouts to talk on watch. Wolz was never one for the strict letter of rules and regulations. But he wanted men keeping watch and looking out, not with half their attention on whatever trivia it was they were chattering about.

He was prepared to be harsh on the matter.

Also, he wanted that sole remaining torpedo to find a good home.

In the guts of a British ship.

A battleship – or an aircraft carrier.

The hydrophones, of the latest model and of an uncanny keenness in detecting underwater sounds, proved troublesome. Perhaps they were just too damned sensitive. Wolz had a word with the operator and all the boat's experts had their various way with the equipment; but it continued refractory.

'See what you can do,' Grunberger said. 'I don't like not being able to hear what's going on.'

'Very good!'

As the operator went off towards his little cubby, Wolz reflected that if the wabos started coming down, they'd all hear what was going on, without any difficulty.

The officers and men of U-112 looked with condescending pity on the two Luftwaffe flyers. Here all the spirit of the U-boat arm could rightfully be expressed. But, all the same, Trojer and Lindemann, once they had overcome their initial sickness, were tolerated as denizens of a strange world momentarily visiting. For Baldur Wolz, the crew of U-112 harboured other and, to Wolz, odd feelings. He wished he could pin down these uneasy sensations, say to himself, outright, that these crewmen detested him because Adolf Forstner had lied to them. But that was too obvious. They treated him with a respect he at first thought feigned, phoney, mocking.

Getting himself ready to go on watch, he pulled on the heavy waterproofs that had to be shared in the boat. Although the stuffy stink of the boat hung all about him and the lighting gleamed brightly, up aloft it was night, and it was going to be cold, wet and miserable on the bridge.

He went through to the control room and glanced up at the hatch to the tower. The time was moving on – the alarm went off and the boat convulsed to life.

The watch above came tumbling down, scattering icy

water drops. The hatch came down with a muffled clang. The diesels chopped off only just in time – the air blew smartly past for a moment or two and Wolz's ears popped.

'Flood! Dive, dive dive!' The yells rang out.

Men cannoned into one another, staggering. The boat put her head down and dived.

Grunberger appeared, demanding to be heard.

'Destroyer, sir. Destroyer – right on top of us. Visibility is bad, very bad –'

'Hold her steady, Chief,' rapped Grunberger.

Wolz stepped back, out of the way. He studied the men's faces, dirty, bearded, sweaty. He saw the black circles under their eyes, the shifty look, and he shook his head. U-112 was not, was most certainly not, a happy boat.

No sounds reached down to them in the depths. Their own hydrophone gear had malfunctioned. The tension held everyone with an indrawn breath. But if the destroyer was as close as the watch said, they would have heard the rapid railway train beat of her screws by now. Silence . . .

They waited. The whites of their eyes showed as they stared up. The steel hull held them imprisoned. And no sound of hostile English destroyers reached down.

When Grunberger felt it to be safe, he ordered periscope depth. He made a long and careful search.

'It's dark and the visibility is bad. But there is no sign –' He hesitated. Wolz could see the strain coming on him. 'Surface!' Grunberger said, with a snap.

When U-112 surfaced and the watch tumbled out, Wolz made sure he was well up at the front, and looking all around the compass. He didn't like the itchy feeling down his back that sailing with this quality of crew gave him. He did not like it at all.

There was no sign of a destroyer, no sign of a ship at all.

Then the discovery was made that Kurt Singer was

missing. He had been one of the lookouts. He had not tumbled down the hatch when the alarm had been raised.

Wolz had heard of cases like this.

'He must have gone to sleep,' raged Grunberger. 'A lookout, asleep at his post.'

'And when we submerged he was simply washed off –'

'There was too much –'

'Yes.'

A man who went to sleep risked not only his own life but the lives of all his crewmates. He would be propped in his position with the binoculars at his eyes, fast asleep. The emergency came, and the boat dived – and he simply got washed away. The lifejacket would support him in the sea; but the cold would kill him stone dead in no time.

Wolz knew many men in the U-boat arm of the Kriegs-marine who would screw their eyebrows down and screw their lips up at the incident and say the navy was well rid of men who slept at their posts, and serve 'em damn well right. The Army shot sentries who went to sleep. The sea could do the job in a less messy fashion for the U-boats.

Was it, Wolz wondered, just the war that could make men think like that? Or were those attitudes merely a private part of their natures, eternal?

He stood his watch and he made very sure that the lookouts stayed awake.

Somewhere out there *Bismarck* was limping along with that tell-tale streak of oil fanning out aft, and the English were gathering. *Bismarck*, the latest and best of battleships, would face a motley collection of ships the English had scraped up. It would be like a great stag of the mountains shaking off a pack of cur dogs, noble and vital and free . . .

Whatever the U-boats could do to help must be done. Sentiment as well as orders dictated that.

Sentiment and orders – well, they might march in har-ness in that connection, but he remembered poor Lottie and the way sentiment and orders conflicted so violently for her. She had been a breezy, happy, reckless girl, with wonderful legs and laughing face and romping ways that could always effortlessly captivate him. Poor Lottie!

The wedding invitation reached him in the most formal way and Lottie had not included a little note on perfumed paper. Wolz had seen clearly the resignation with which she faced up to this arranged marriage when he'd spent that fraught twenty minutes with her in the railway carriage standing in the station.

'I might have to marry some red-necked fat oaf in a munitions plant – something to do with bringing the two families together. Father is worn out.'

That was what Lottie had told him, and the truth of her words was neatly printed in his hands.

Cousin Helmut, who was Gestapo, was unable to get away to attend the wedding. Cousin Siegfried, who was SS, also could not get away, and Wolz gathered with pleasure that Siegfried was much involved with Marlene again. As for Cousin Manfred, there had been a ground loop. Bf109s notoriously handled badly on the ground, and Manfred had, apparently, written off a couple of trucks, a parked communications aeroplane and narrowly missed depriving the Staffel of its commander. Manfred, too, would not be going to the wedding.

The honour of the Wolz family, therefore, was left in Baldur Wolz's naval hands.

The armaments family into which Lottie was marrying so as to form a combine to produce more guns and tanks for the Third Reich put on a good show. Lottie's father did not look well. He appeared crushed. As for Lottie, there was no sign of her as Wolz went into the ancestral home, bowered in trees and with the west wing in imminent danger of falling down. Orders for armaments had been cut; but all the talk among the gathered guests was of a fresh spate of orders, of the wheels turning again, and of a much more happy future. The guests presented a useful cross-section of German upper society, those who were in the know, those who had the money and power, and those like Wolz himself who did the fighting.

He fell into conversation with an infantry Major and a weak-chested and eye-glassed man who was something to do with petro-chemicals. Their conversation was a mass of cliché and small talk and Wolz was bored to the back teeth.

He excused himself and went off to reconnoitre the champagne situation.

Wolz had seen caricatures of Prussians in English magazines. The Square Heads, with the cropped brush bristle sharp across the head, the neck ridged straight up and down, the monocle, the duelling scar. This Friedrich Stallmann Lottie was marrying might have posed for the caricature.

Wolz had to fight an instinctive dislike as they shook hands.

Stallmann said: 'Lottie has told me nothing of you, Herr Wolz. You are in the services, of course? Alas, I am far too important producing the weapons to fight with to go and use them in action, much though I would dearly love to do so.'

'Yes—'

'My younger brother would have gone into the Luftwaffe; but he is too valuable as my assistant. You really have no idea of my problems. I hardly ever have time to rest. The armaments ministry is always telephoning, night and day.'

'I'm sure—'

'Please find some champagne. I have enjoyed our talk. Perhaps we can continue later, but—' His eyeglass glittered. He beamed at a short stout man in a frock coat. 'Herr Professor, how good to see you! Come along and—' He went off with the Herr Professor, and Wolz stared after them and had to fight hard not to burst out laughing.

The wedding itself did not quite put him to sleep. Lottie robed in white stood like a marble statue—trite words but true, too damned true. Wolz didn't like the look of her at all. She looked like a dough-figure waiting to be popped into the oven.

Her friend Heidi – who was by way of being a friend and a romp to Wolz, also – was there and she had been crying.

The ceremony ended and as the guests started in on the important drinking part of the procedings, the happy couple circulated. Wolz had heard they were to leave by midnight and he made himself scarce. He just couldn't face Stallmann again, and he didn't care to see Lottie like this. He'd have a private word with her before she left. But he sensed he might so easily make matters worse.

The speeches were declaimed in a heavy pompous fashion and the drink flowed and Wolz wandered off to the upper floors and saw the door to the ruined west wing. A maid with frightened eyes scurried past, half-curtseying. Wolz gave her a smile and waited quietly until she had gone down the black-polished stairs past the stag-heads and the harnesses of armour.

The noise from below reached up like the sea on a rocky shore. He mentally upped his periscope and pushed the door to the west wing open. The place was musty, filled with cobwebs and shadows, most of the windows boarded over.

He went through into the long dusty hall.

Out of affection for Lottie he had come to her wedding. That had been a mistake. As soon as he decently could he would excuse himself and leave.

In the old days there would have been a gigantic ceremony in the cathedral, with choirs and the organ and the whole works. Girls, these days, missed a deal of what was theirs. The place up here smelled of byegone days, of tall wax candles and perfumes, of horse liniment and harness polish and saddle soap. These days the acrid stinks of gunsmoke and petrol dominated people's horizons.

He heard the swift scuffle and turned.

'Baldur! Oh, Baldur!'

She came into his arms in a whirl of loosened hair, of sweet perfume and of tears.

'Lottie –'

'Baldur – it's horrible. I don't know what I'm to do.'

'You're married now.'

'Yes. Isn't it vile? Have you a cigarette?'

'No.'

'Your manners are as pleasant as ever –'

'You may have a cigar, with great pleasure.'

'Oh, Baldur!' She kissed him, hot and moist and sweet. 'Mitzi told me you were in here, wandering off like a lost loon. Just like you.' Mitzi must have been the maid. 'I must change. Come back with me. I'm dying for – for a cigarette.'

He followed her back out of the doorway and along the landing. The noise from below bellowed up. They crept noiselessly along the carpet and Lottie beckoned him into her room. The place was strewn with clothes like a rummage sale.

She found her cigarettes and lit up and then flopped down on a divan and stuck her legs out. She hauled her skirt up to her knees, and puffed smoke, and lay back, closing her eyes.

'What am I to do, Baldur?'

'This Stallmann –'

'You've seen him? He'll be like a Hamburg butcher.'

'You can handle him. Why, Lottie, one sight –'

'Yes, yes. I'll handle the bastard. But tonight, Baldur, tonight!'

'I see.'

'Do you?'

'We-ell. Let's say I see some of it. It all depends on your own willpower.'

'That's it, Baldur. I'll have to bridle and saddle him from the word go.'

'That's the idea. Anyway, he was telling me how important and busy he is.'

She laughed.

'Busy! I'll see he's busy. I'll get a French maid – she ought to dampen down the fires – if there are any.'

Wolz stood by the divan. Lottie opened her eyes and stared up at him. She did look drawn.

'I have to change and then we're away at midnight. But you know. I must change –'

She stood up and Wolz went across and helped her out of her dress. She wore a white slip. Her white stockings looked odd to Wolz, accustomed to seeing Lottie's slender tapering legs encased in sheer black silk.

Lottie licked her lips. She threw her cigarette into the fireplace. 'We have time, Baldur –'

'Your wedding dress –'

'That will add something.'

'True.'

Her brassiere was a mere white slinky lacework and she threw it at his head in the old style. He caught it, feeling the silkiness, and then threw it back. She laughed.

'Oh, Baldur – just think! I've missed you so, and now it's going to be ever so much worse. Stallmann is –'

'Forget Stallmann. Come here.'

The noise of the celebration from below reached in a muffled uproar through the door. Lottie came into his arms, warm and soft and altogether lovely. He kissed her and she kissed him back. He could feel her body against his. The divan proved temptingly available. Her hands moved with their old assurance.

'Just think, Baldur. I shall be doing this tonight – with him!'

'Concentrate on what you're doing now.'

She gasped. He felt her arms clutch him desperately.

'I shall think of this moment tonight –'

He smiled and stroked her and she sighed with a transient happiness.

'Now, Baldur, I must fly! Stallmann will be waiting –'

She held a scrap of her wedding gown against her naked body and eased the door open with her other hand. She peeked and instantly shut the door, silently.

'Baldur! They're out there, on the landing at the head of the stairs. Talking and smoking and laughing – and Stallmann is with them.'

'Then I cannot possibly leave.'

'And Mitzi will be in any moment –'

Wolz walked to the window. It was set deeply in a stone embrasure and it made an infernal noise opening. The night wind slapped in. He shivered.

'But it is too far up!'

'There is a ledge. Now, Lottie, listen and remember. You are a wonderful girl, and we've had some fun times. But you are married now. You've a great deal to live for –'

'Nonsense, Baldur!'

'No, it's true. I'll see you when I'm on leave, if I can.'

'Promise?'

'I promise.'

He put a foot on the stone ledge. It was a damned long way down.

A light knock sounded on the door.

'That's Mitzi! Baldur . . .'

Wolz put his other leg through the opening and sat sideways. He groped down for the ledge. The wind whistled up his trousers.

'Baldur – don't go! I don't care. I'll get Mitzi in, there'll be the most frightful row, and then it'll all be over –'

'Lottie! Think straight, old girl. That would only mess it all up. I will see you, I promised, and you'll find you'll get to like marriage –'

'Stuff and nonsense! You've seen Stallmann.'

'Shut your eyes –'

'– and think of tonight, of now, of the divan – of all the other times –'

'Goodbye, Lottie. It'll all turn out all right, you'll see.'

The knock came again and Lottie called, crossly, that she was coming. Wolz found the ledge and, with a quick shuffle, trusted his weight to it. It did not give way.

He was out of the window and Lottie was hauling it shut as he pushed. His last glimpse of her was as, reaching up for the metal handle, she raised her arms. The scrap of wedding gown fell away. She was limned in half-sil-houette, taut, stretched, and yet looking as though he was abandoning her – and he wasn't, it wasn't fair, it wasn't like that. Lottie was Lottie, a good romp and that was all they had meant to each other.

He shinnied along the ledge in a furious rage, and found some cracks and ivy, and cornices, and odds and ends of the architects' and builders' trades and so dropped silently to the grass. It was cold and the wind was now howling mournfully and he went back in smartly enough and found himself some schnapps.

Presently the men's conversation once more bored him. When everyone joined together for the last orgiastic ex-hibition of emotion as the lucky bride and groom de-parted amid a mass of waving handkerchiefs and tears, Wolz shook his head in wonder at the weather-vane mentality of the human spirit, and went back for the schnapps. Heidi, as cheeky and voluptuous as ever, found him after a time, and it was diving stations and flood all tanks and up periscope for another romp or two.

As the filthy Atlantic weather slapped him in the face, and his red-rimmed eyes felt full of grit, and his arms and legs ached with the motion, and yet he continued to look out and make sure the watch looked out also, he re-flected that those times helped to make these times that much more bearable.

Wolz spotted the Swordfish first.

His yell and the resultant immediate clearing of the bridge was followed by U-112's crash dive in to the depths. The U-boat went down with a rush. As she levelled off at a safe depth, Wolz realised what that Swordfish meant.

Somewhere near them was an English aircraft carrier.

And that carrier was hunting Bismarck.

Now – U-112 would go hunting the hunter.

CHAPTER TWELVE

Admiral Raeder had persuaded Hitler to go to Gdynia and give an encouraging patriotic address to the companies of the two warships involved in Rheinübung. *Bismarck* and *Prinz Eugen* would clear the high seas of English shipping. Everything that flew the Red or White Ensign they met would be sent to the bottom. This was in fulfilment of the manifest destiny of the German race. Heil Hitler!

Now *Prinz Eugen* was scuttling with contaminated fuel for safety, and *Bismarck*, crippled, awaited the end after a night of flame and terror. The five destroyers of the Fourth Flotilla commanded by Captain Vian had badgered and harried and torpedoed the massive battleship all through the hours of darkness as *King George V* and *Rodney* of the Home Fleet steamed on an intercept course. The eight-inch cruisers, *Norfolk* and *Dorsetshire*, held the ring on the flanks, and Force H lay over the horizon.

In U-112, normal routine went on in a hushed, almost furtive way. The dawn was a wild affair, with a half gale from the nor' west and the sea breaking and scudding. Occasional squalls of rain blew in sudden fierce gusts. The clouds hung low, dark and full-bellied, and cast an eerie shadow over the sea.

Wolz stared across that dismal waste of tumbled water. Grunberger had been taking in Commander Only signals, and had passed out scraps of information. What was known was the desperate situation of *Bismarck*, of Admiral Lütjens' plea for assistance from the U-boats and the Luftwaffe.

As Hauptmann Trojer said, shaking his head and looking savage: 'Outside the range of our aircraft. A gruppe of JU88s is needed, and, if they could get here, some Stukas. Maybe they'd sink enough English ships – '

Lindemann looked sick. 'Why can't you U-boat men sink the English battleships?'

Grunberger's eyes were deeply sunk in his head. He was, like them all, filthy. A U-boat carried two sorts of water – drinking water and washing water – and they were not washing and were drinking the washing water sweetened into a foul mess by syrup. The torpedomen would be at the eels soon to draw off the water there if they weren't watched. Grunberger had the key of the water tap in the galley safely in his pocket.

'They are out of torpedoes, Herr Hauptmann. And most are almost out of fuel.'

'We,' Wolz had said. 'Have one eel.'

Grunberger's eyes slid away like eggs in a greasy frying pan.

He did not make any reply

So; now Wolz was on the bridge and looking across the empty sea against the drizzle and the grey overcast and hurting himself for the sight of an English ship.

He itched with the desire to bathe and wash himself clean. Officers were supposed to be able to wash in washing water, whilst the ratings washed in salt water with special salt-water soap. But water was short and the end of the patrol nowhere in sight. Forstner had this to answer for as well as the rest of his sins.

When Wolz went down the conning tower ladder into the control room he felt the fug hit him like a hobnailed boot in the face. Nothing was dry. Everything reeked with mould and dampness and stink. Even the coffee tasted foul.

No one was in the mood to speak. The boat was fractious this morning; the LI was having some difficulty in holding a trim. No one was permitted to move about the boat without orders.

Wolz felt more strongly than ever how much in the way he was in U-112. With the two Luftwaffe men he tried to play a game of cards; but the pasteboards were peeling and unpleasantly slick in the fingers. The cook – whom everyone called Smutje – was boiling up some indescribable muck. The air gave out headaches for free. The hydrophones refused to work. And B.d.U. had no solace for anyone – continue patrol and report any enemy activity.

The Elektro Obermaschinist reported that he suspected a crack in one of the batteries – and Grunberger screamed at him, berating him mercilessly. If there was a crack and the acid got into the seawater in the bilges among the rats – Wolz shut his mind away from that. U-112 had a job to do and would do it, and she'd make her way back to base. If she had to crawl there on her hands and knees.

They were about four hundred and twenty miles west of Brest and St. Nazaire. Wolz wondered what the signals that kept coming in from B.d.U. contained. *Bismarck* ought to be steaming hell for leather for safety – the English with the loss of *Hood* to spur them on would be ravening at the German battleship's heels.

Just what in hell's name was going on?

When the alarm screamed and U-112 dived, Wolz was into the control room feeling the headache ready to burst out through his skull. The watch tumbled down the ladder and the U-boat put her head down. Grunberger held her at fourteen metres and the LJ trimmed her off.

'Up periscope.'

'Up periscope.'

This was the sky search scope, and Grunberger snapped the handles and looked carefully around the compass before lowering the spargel.

He looked at Wolz.

Wolz's hard face betrayed no emotion. His grimy, lined features held that look that could make the men jump. His blue eyes bored into Grunberger.

'A Swordfish –'

'That means the carrier is still around. No signs of *Bismarck* or the English?'

'No.'

A signal had come in at seven o'clock from B.d.U. but Wolz had not been told its contents.

Even beneath the surface U-112 rolled and heaved to the weather aloft. It was foul up there. The LI kept on raging at the planesmen to keep the boat level and he was continually flooding and blowing to keep a trim. Wolz just didn't like any of this.

He looked steadily at Grunberger. The temporary commander had made no effort to raise the periscope again. With the hydrophones out of action U-112 was deaf beneath the sea.

'Permission to take a look? Herr Oberleutnant?'

Grunberger licked his lips again.

Then, almost pettishly, he said: 'Very well.' He half-turned away and said over his shoulder. 'For all the good it will do you.'

'Up periscope!'

'Up periscope!'

Wolz jammed his eye against the rubber eyepiece. It was slick and unpleasant; but he ignored that. He twisted the grips, tilting the lens, and carried out a swift 360 degree sea and sky search.

Nothing. About to order down periscope he halted. There, at the limit of vision, sweeping away beyond a rain squall – was that a dark outline? No aircraft were in the sky and no destroyers bore down on him. He could take another heartbeat to look – the periscope cut under and all he could see was green and foaming water.

'Down periscope. Chief! Can't you hold a trim?'

'It's rough up there –'

'It's rough up there, Herr Oberleutnant! You'll hold her or I'll have your guts out! Up periscope!'

This time the shape was there, dark and unmistakable.

He slammed the spargel down and turned to Grunberger.

He spoke passionlessly, his words cold and metallic.

'There's a battleship up there. King George V class.'

'Impossible!'

'Look for yourself, Herr Oberleutnant.'

Grunberger's face slicked in the overheads. A muscle leaped alongside his jaw. He looked a sick man. Well, they all looked sick men.

'Up periscope!'

This time Grunberger looked out on the bearing Wolz provided. When the telescope hissed down into its well Grunberger looked sicker still.

'Well?'

'There is a ship – but I am not convinced it is a King George V – that could be *Bismarck*.'

'Two funnels, single turret aft –'

'Yes, yes!'

'Our duty –'

'I know my duty and do not need to be reminded of it.'

Wolz shut his mouth, stared implacably at Grunberger – and waited.

The atmosphere in the boat stank. It stank of other essences than cabbage and fuel and pitch and urine. It stank of fear.

Fear was an old companion as far as Wolz and the men of the U-boats were concerned. It had to be figured into the calculations. It had to be made use of.

Wolz waited.

He would wait for just so long – and then he would act and risk a court martial.

The air lines in U-boats always leaked just that trifle to bring the interior air-pressure up above atmospheric pressure. Wolz seemed to be able to feel that pressure working on him, driving into his head, forcing in his ear drums. He could feel the weight on his chest. It was all in his imagination, of course. The difference was noticeable when the hatch was flung open and the pressures equalised. Then the old ears popped.

Now he stared malevolently at Grunberger. The temporary skipper's lips were white. He chewed on one of those bloodless lips like a terrier worrying a slipper. He could not meet Wolz's eyes.

The Second Watch Officer kept out of it, and the Chief busied himself in the cluttered background. The maze of pipes and valves and levers and dials shone and glittered in the lighting. The boat stank. The harsh sound of Grunberger's breathing cut through like a reaping machine among the high stalks of corn.

At last Grunberger said: 'Kapitänleutnant Adolf Forstner would have known the correct procedure. If we go up the English will –' Again he chewed his flaccid lip. 'It is certain death to go up – surely you can see that.'

'Maybe it is. But *Bismarck* –'

'*Bismarck* is doomed!'

Wolz wouldn't stand any more of this. He cocked an eye up.

The quartermaster in the tower and the torpedo director rating – who waited stolidly for orders – would have to be witnesses. Regulations meant to Baldur Wolz a way of getting things done. If that way conflicted with what he considered the right way, then he was still not prepared to compromise what he believed in for the sake of regulations.

He had to measure his own career against the fate of a battleship and the lives of two thousand men.

Even if he failed, he would have done what he could. Anything less was not good enough for Baldur Wolz. And yet he saw the futility of his own actions and could see how he was throwing away his prospects – and yet he could do nothing less.

'Will you order an attack, Herr Oberleutnant?'

'Against what? The whole English fleet?'

Wolz struggled to keep his composure. What was said and done would all be raked over at the court martial.

'Our duty as naval officers of the Kriegsmarine is to go in to the attack. You say *Bismarck* is doomed. I do not know that – '

'B.d.U. signalled! All U-boats with torpedoes are to proceed towards *Bismarck* at full speed – well, we tried. But you know the state of the sea – '

'And the other signals?'

The remorseless tones unnerved Grunberger even more. He looked down at the deck and the greasy wetness, and he would not meet Wolz's eyes.

'U-556 has been ordered to take off *Bismarck*'s log – '

Now Wolz understood why Grunberger said the battleship was doomed. Only a captain expecting his ship to be sunk would make a signal requesting his log to be taken to safety.

'All that means nothing beside our duty,' he said. 'You and I both know that, Grunberger. We are going up.'

'No!'

Wolz called up into the tower and told the torpedo director rating to come down. The man showed the whites of his eyes as he scuttled down and through the control room. Wolz said to Grunberger: 'Come up into the tower, Herr Oberleutnant. We can talk more freely there.'

'But – '

'We need to – talk.'

In the tower Wolz glared balefully at the helmsman.

'Obersteuermann – shut your ears, concentrate on your helm. You see and hear nothing. Understood?'

'Very good!'

Then Wolz turned to Grunberger.

He did not try one last time. He made no last plea. In the cramped space the blow was difficult to deliver with accuracy as well as force; but Baldur Wolz was wrought up. He hit Grunberger flush alongside the jaw and did not catch him as he went down. His head cracked against the attack periscope. He doubled up, crumpled, unable to flop out.

Wolz bellowed down into the control room.

'Stabsoberbootsmann! Come up here and help with the

commander. He has fallen and cracked his head. Treat him gently!'

'Very good.'

The cox'n's voice held a note of doubt and uncertainty. Little red flecks danced before Wolz's eyes.

He showed a face of unremitting ferocity to the cox'n, and that worthy, conscious of his rank, hurriedly organised a party to bring the commander out of the tower.

Grunberger's face looked waxed, shiny and polished. He breathed in stertorous gasps. His lips, now, were purple.

'Get him into his cabin. Then stand by action stations. Jump!'

'Very good.'

As Grunberger was carried away, Wolz gave the orders he deemed necessary. Prepare and flood the aft tube. Men at action stations. The hydrophones were useless, and he felt like a rat in a trap with mufflers over his ears. But when he upped the scope and looked, everything else fell away in importance.

He had attempted to take this whole affair as quietly as possible, without dramatics. And certainly without heroics. If this was mutiny then he wanted it in low key, quiet, unobtrusive. Grunberger had fallen and hit his head. That was common enough in U-boats. If anything else was made of it afterwards . . .

Well, there might not be any afterwards.

For all the Sanitatsobermaat was doing for Grunberger's two nasty cracks – the one on the back of his head was easily explicable. The bruise alongside his jaw, should the Herr Oberleutnant wish to take the matter any further, might call for more specious explanations. The truth would hardly be believed.

'Up periscope!'

The scope went up, Wolz twirled the handles, and –

'Down periscope!'

The English destroyer was not quite on top of them but she was dangerously close. The bone in her teeth spouted up over her forecastle. The sea raged up there. The destroyer roared past to starboard and everyone heard the quick rattle of her screws. Wolz felt all his nerve-endings responding. He could plan the positions of U-112, the destroyer, the distant battleship, plot them off in his head.

He took another fast look, the spargel just going up and down on the bearing.

She was a Tribal and she was going fast. No pings from her underwater detection apparatus sounded, and Wolz suspected she was not searching for U-boats. She was going too fast for that and in this weather she was almost as much under the water as the U-boat herself.

The English did not generally use Tribal class fleet destroyers on convoy duty. That beauty had been having a go at *Bismarck*.

The screw effect faded and vanished. Wolz took another look around the compass.

Rain squalls beat across his vision. The sky hung murkily over the churned surface of the sea.

Directly before him two tall columns stood up in the sea. He blinked. White, shining, like ice-covered Christmas trees, they stood suddenly up from the sea, broadened, expanded, fell away whipped by the half-gale.

Wolz knew what those waterspouts were.

They were close enough for the underwater shock of the shells' explosions to reach U-112 and gong against her hull . . .

Someone below shouted: 'Wabos!'

'Silence, that man!' bellowed Wolz. 'They—'

Two more thuds boomed against U-112's plates.

Wolz took another look.

This time—this time he saw what the rain squalls had been hiding . . .

Rheinübung was drawing to a close in an inferno of fire . . .

The positions of the ships involved sprang into Wolz's brain. The English battleships were shooting, the destroyers were hauling out of it, and, directly before his appalled gaze she lay, black and low in the water, riddled, sieved, her upperworks gone, and fires spouting from her in licking tongues of evil flame and black belches of smoke.

Bismarck – shot to pieces, sinking , doomed . . .

The periscope came down. Wolz sat on the saddle seat and for a moment he could see nothing but that gruesome picture flickering in his mind. Like a black log. Like a burning log in a fireplace. Like a huddled corpse tossed on the funeral pyre. *Bismarck* – destroyed.

He roused himself.

There was a single eel left in his stern tube and there were English ships up there.

The equation was obvious.

Courses could be given and fed into the attack table. Corrections could be made. Speeds could be maintained. All the usual procedures for a successful attack could be taken.

But Wolz was aware that U-112 was not a happy boat.

Things that could go wrong would go wrong. The crew were discontented, borne down by the weight of the privations they suffered as all U-boat men suffered. But in a happy boat, in an efficient boat – in a boat like his own U-55 – the weight of hardship forged by its hammer blows a fiercer temper. The men responded so as to show that they could rise above hardship and danger.

In U-112 Wolz was darkly aware that he must shoulder the burdens himself. It was down to him and to him alone to carry this through. And – he doubted. He doubted that U-112 was capable of what he demanded.

If anything could go wrong – it would go wrong.

He sensed that, he knew that, and he could only hope that his professional expertise in seeing all too clearly the lamentable uselessness of U-112 was at fault.

But he did not think it was.

The courses were followed. The boat managed to reach four knots submerged and they would not keep that up for too long. He took another look at *Bismarck*. He decided that the time to tell the crew of the disaster would be later.

The English shelling faded and died.

U-112, a steel shark with rotten fangs, glided on under the surface.

Twice the heavy beat of racing screws passed away to the side and on both occasions Wolz did not dive but calmly watched as the Tribals sped past.

When he checked again a high-hulled, three-funnelled cruiser steamed into his vision. He watched, savagely unable to affect the course of that battle. She was a County class. With eight eight-inch guns, she was armoured in silver paper; but she was fast enough. An eel into her side plates would send her to the bottom. But she glided past well out of range, and Wolz continued doggedly to plod on after the bigger game.

When the next check time came around the Chief just couldn't hold the boat in trim. The scope kept cutting under. Furiously, Wolz said : 'Down periscope. Chief. I shall have to send in an adverse report if this goes on. Is there anything seriously wrong with the boat? If so, it is your duty to inform me.'

'Yes, Herr Oberleutnant. But – '

Wolz hammered a fist on to the cold metal.

'Hold her in trim, Chief, or I'll put a boot into your backside.'

Although unable to see the crew from his saddle seat in the tower, Wolz was unpleasantly aware that few, if any of them would hide a smirk at his words. They were beaten down. Even that little spectacle would not rouse the spirit in them. Their faces would remain as blank and filthy as coal-house doors.

What the LI was up to in the control room and what he was saying to his engineering personnel, Wolz neither knew nor cared. He wanted a U-boat that would run and which did not keep dunking her spargel.

'Up periscope!'

'Up periscope.'

This time the lens broke free of the crested wavetops and gave him a view that persisted as a dream-sequence, a view for which any U-boat officer prayed to all the gods of the undersea.

Close, less than two thousand metres, and rising like the wall of a block of flats, the grey hull and massive citadel of a Nelson class battleship . . .

Wolz licked his lips.

He slammed the scope down and then checked with the aft torpedo room that everything was ready. He checked with the attack table. He checked the Chief. He had no need to check himself. He knew what had to be done, and he would do it.

He gave a couple more quick observations to determine the utmost accuracy of the attack. The angle was coming off nicely. The English battleship was steaming directly on to the correct bearing aft and when the moment came he could loose the eel directly into her. Point of aim — engine room.

If there was any miscalculation, if the rough sea interfered with the dead run of the eel, then the torpedo would have the length of that massive hull into which to plunge and bite. A shrewd blow around the screws and the rudder . . . That was where the English Swordfish had torpedoed *Bismarck*.

The time came down remorselessly. His throat felt dry. A quick survey showed no destroyers. Without the hydrophones they'd never be heard until they were right on top of U-112.

He tensed and forced himself to relax.

The moment came — a hand reached out and clutched his leg. He looked down, shocked.

Grunberger, his face like chalk, his eyes like black pits, glared exhaustedly at him.

'You — Wolz —' Grunberger swallowed. 'Come on — down.'

Wolz kicked.

Grunberger held on.

'You're under arrest!' he screamed.

'Not until I've put this eel into the battleship—'

'Madman! You'll get us all killed!'

Grunberger was screaming now, the redness of his mouth shocking against the pallor and grime of his face.

Suddenly, Grunberger released Wolz's leg. He vanished. There were shouts from below and harsh bellows.

U-112 began to dive.

Before Wolz could yell he felt the soggy thump and the hiss of compressed air. The Chief flooded to compensate for the lost weight.

Where the torpedo had gone, Wolz did not know.

What he did know was that it had gone nowhere near the English battleship.

He dropped down through the hatch into the conning tower in such a rage the muscles alongside his jaw bulged.

'You idiot!' he bellowed. 'You cretin! You've lost us that battleship—'

Grunberger looked ghastly.

He panted. 'There will be a court martial! You are under arrest! I'll have you hanged for this—'

'And I'll have you dismissed the service! You lamebrain! The eel was dead on, dead to rights—and you—you—'

The smashing concussion shocked through the boat. Lights went out. They staggered wildly and some men fell screaming to the deck. Others caught hold of anything to hand, hanging on as more deadly concussions blasted through the water. The noise hammered and reverberated in U-112's pressure hull.

The glass of the gauges broke. Water spat viciously from fractured pipes. The stink and the noise, the dim blue emergency lighting, the shrieks of injured men, built into a pandemonium.

Again the boat shook like a bone in the teeth of a terrier.

The depth charges rained down around them.

'Dive! Take her down!'

U-112 dropped into the deeper depths pursued by the ominous crash and thud of exploding depth charges.

'Report damage!' yelled Wolz.

He hauled himself upright and bellowed the men back to their positions. New bulbs were being screwed in. The next pattern of charges exploded at such a distance that the boat merely rocked, swaying in the depths.

Another pattern tumbled down, and this time their ears picked up the bursts as harsh metallic thunderclaps. Wolz gulped a breath.

'They're dropping blind. They can't pick us up in this weather. Silent routine. Quarter speed on the port motor.'

'No, no!' There was foam on Grunberger's lips. 'Full speed on both motors. Let us get away –'

Wolz moved across. He stared at Grunberger.

'You have been relieved of command, Herr Oberleutnant. Please be quiet –'

'You're under arrest! You can't –'

Wolz swung to the cox'n.

'Stabsoberbootsman! The Herr Oberleutnant is not well. You will place him under restraint at once.'

As Meckel eased his big bear-like shoulders, quite at a loss and not knowing what to do, Wolz rode in again, harsh, dominating, completely devoid of mercy.

'Jump, Meckel! This is no play-acting. If we run away at top speed we'll make so much noise they'll hear us in Whitehall. Do as you're told or you'll be back as a matrose! Jump!'

'Very good!'

Grunberger was wailing and cawing with hideous sounds bursting from his throat. His eyes were wild. Wolz pushed him gently towards the wardroom.

'Go along with Meckel. And take a pill – or three. We'll get out of this alive.'

As he spoke so the distant echo of exploding wabos drifted in, faint and harmless.

The cox'n shepherded Grunberger away. Wolz turned

his baleful eyes upon the control room. They looked once, and then every eye looked away.

Partially satisfied, Baldur Wolz concentrated on nursing U-112 away from this unhealthy neighbourhood. Without hydrophones, with empty tubes, U-112 was now a liability in the continuing war at sea.

Whatever the outcome of the fracas, he'd fight for what he believed in. If Grunberger preferred charges, then Wolz would counter-charge. He'd produce damning evidence if the crewmen spoke the truth. If Adolf Forstner's pervasive influence persisted beyond the grave, why, then he'd be in for a rough ride.

It would all be decided when they returned to Lorient.

Lorient. That's where he'd take U-112. He'd be among his own flotilla, then, and he felt he could guarantee himself a fair hearing.

The U-boat arm could do without men like Forstner and boats like U-112.

Bismarck had gone and they had wasted their last eel and he felt the savage anger at that.

The big destroyers up there were not your small, lumpy, escort destroyers who would hang around a sub-contact past the time when reasonable men should pack up and rejoin the convoy. Wolz heard the distant, booming echo of wabos, and half-smiled. The crew of U-112 had been badly shaken up. He fancied it was their first time under depth charge attack. Well, given the way of the war, it would not be their last.

Presently the sea around them continued as silent as the grave. Wolz stirred himself. He waited for a while longer, and then he gave the order to bring the boat to periscope depth. There would be a melancholy duty in seeing if any men had survived the destruction of *Bismarck*. Only when he had carried out that task would he set course for base.

They would reach Lorient. Wolz had no doubts on that.

And then?

Why, then—it was not written in his stars but in the swirling disturbed water as a U-boat flooded and dived—he'd take his faithful old U-55 out on patrol again.

What more fitting way was there for a U-boatman to return from a reconnaissance flight in a Focke Wulf Kondor than in a U-boat?

That would raise a few eyebrows when he returned to Lorient.

He found himself, suddenly, hungrily, longing for the sight of green fields and trees and the blue unhurried sky.

And then, after that, after a few delightful romps—U-55 was waiting for him.

The U-boats would always be waiting for him.